Irish Ghost Stories & Mysteries from County Down

Written by Annaclone Historical Society

Copyright © 2014 by Annaclone Historical Society

Published by Michael Wallace
Printed in Northern Ireland by WG Baird
First Printing, 2014

ISBN 978-0-9927637-1-8

Lisnavaghrog House
30 Mayscorner Road
Katesbridge
BT32 5RB
www.annaclonehistory.com

Contents

Foreword

"The Supernatural is the natural not yet understood"

Elbert Bubbard (1856-1915)

Ireland has a rich history of ghost, banshee and fairy sightings all around the country and County Down is no exception.

Ghosts may take the form of phantom white or blue ladies, ghostly nuns, children, animals and horse-drawn carriages. Other ghosts make their presence felt through unexplained lights or noises which occur in haunted houses. Ghostly happenings occur in castles, cottages or even open spaces.

Many years ago when there was no electricity, television or the internet, people would gather in their cottages and over a turf fire tell stories and legends about Celtic heroes such as Cuchulain and mythological people such as the Tuatha De Danaan. In rural areas, stories were also told about ghostly sightings, fairies, leprechauns, witches and the dreaded banshee. Every part of Ireland has its own collection of individual tales and mysterious happenings. These stories were handed down over generations. 'Kitty the Hare' ghost stories were very popular in the publication 'Ireland's Own'

This is the second compilation of such stories from Annaclone Historical Society. Our first book 'The Unexplained in Co. Down', published in 2011 sold out within a short period of time and is now out of print. Due to its success, the society decided to collate further stories and publish a second book and have included a limited number of stories from the first one. However, the vast majority of the stories will be new to the reader.

This publication focuses on County Down and areas which border the county for example Carlingford, County Armagh and Belfast. Once again we have concentrated on stories about people who have experienced paranormal activity in one form or another allowing the reader to experience these personal accounts first hand. Other stories have been passed down over the years by word of mouth or have been unearthed during research of old books and newspapers.

Our publication covers haunted buildings and places including Greencastle, the former sites of Downpatrick and Belfast Workhouses and haunted houses in Castlewellan, Annaclone, Ardglass and Banbridge. Our fairy stories range from fairy trees in the Mournes, sightings of fairy people in Hilltown and the Pooka from Kilkeel. We also provide stories of the dreaded banshee, the witch hare and devil related tales from across the county. We journey back in time to retell the story of the Lough Shannagh monster and the 'Fairy Cat' from Clough. Finally, we have included some of the strange and mysterious stories that we came across in our research. Stories that will fascinate you including the disappearance of a daughter in Katesbridge that was widely reported in newspapers across Britain and Ireland in 1868, the surprising number of centenarians in County Down during the 20th Century and severe weather conditions that prevailed back in history.

Even though the tradition of storytelling in modern Ireland has dwindled, there is still a fascination with ghost and fairy stories and mysteries. We hope that this publication will re-generate further interest in the 'Other Ireland' and rekindle the tradition of storytelling. The authors would like to thank all who contributed or assisted in any way with this publication. Our thanks also to the staff in Banbridge and Downpatrick Libraries.

As you read through the book, we would ask the reader "Are you a believer or a sceptic?" Whether you are a believer or not, remember that most of these stories originated from first-hand accounts and many of the people who told us the stories did not believe in ghosts either. However, as the saying goes, 'seeing is believing' so always remember to be on the look-out as you never know what might be lurking in the shadows. You might even feature in our next book!

This is a real image of ghost taken in Belfast

A ghost rider in the mist. Always be careful when you're out for a walk!!

Chapter 1

Haunted Buildings

Inch Abbey, Downpatrick

The Blue Nun of Ardnabannon House

Ardnabannon House is in Castlewellan and was built by the Architect Thomas Turner for Charles Murland (1820-1887). Charles was the youngest son of James Murland who was responsible for the expansion of the Murland business during the nineteenth century.

In 1967, the house was purchased by the Down County Education Committee and converted into an Outdoor Pursuits Centre. The west corridor of the house is said to be haunted.

The story originates from the family house which previously occupied the site. This former manor house was owned by a wealthy Castlewellan family who only had one son who was destined to inherit the family estate. However, the story goes that he fell in love with a nun from a nearby convent. His family were outraged at this; for one of them to marry a former nun would bring shame on them and tarnish their reputation.

During the next winter, they decided to take matters into their own hands and kidnapped the nun. While the snow lay on the ground they then tied her up in the grounds of their manor house and left her there exposed to the freezing temperatures. The nun died of hypothermia and was found blue with the cold. That is why her ghost is referred to as the 'blue nun' as she continues to haunt the corridors of Ardnabannon House forever searching for her long dead love. The clinking sound heard is that of the chains in which she was tied up.

Many school children claim to have seen the ghost while they have stayed in the house on an Outdoor Pursuits break.

The Ghosts of Downpatrick, Banbridge & Belfast Workhouses

Downpatrick Workhouse was built in 1842 and consisted of a three storey building. It housed many poor unfortunate people, young and old and many died there during the famine years. Hundreds of unknown paupers were buried in a field situated behind the workhouse. The former workhouse has long since been demolished but prior to that it was used for a time as a leather factory after the Second World War.

Many of the workers in the leather factory would experience strange happenings, unexplained noises and changes in temperature. One day a worker was in the store when he felt a chill and a tingling of the hairs on the back of his neck. He turned round and noticed a small old man wearing an old fashioned flat cap walk across the room and suddenly disappear at one of the windows. The workman was so frightened that he rushed from the store and refused to go back inside unless someone else came with him. The following day, news came to the factory that a former workhouse employee had died and his description fitted that of the ghostly figure seen in the storeroom.

Once during the night shift, workers heard noises coming from the second floor of the factory. Thinking it was burglars, they rushed upstairs. They observed a door at the end of one of the corridors lying open but there was no-one about. Just then another door opened at the opposite end of the same corridor and a door in the middle also opened. The men searched the whole area but could find no-one. Eventually, they believed that the only explanation for the strange happening was that the ghosts of the workhouse were causing the doors to open.

Another story relating to the workhouse involves a local lady who once observed a little girl dressed in Victorian clothes and standing close by the old workhouse building. Thinking she needed help to cross the road, the lady stopped her car but as she got out and looked back, the little girl had disappeared.

There have been numerous sightings of ghosts walking around the grounds and on the road near the site of the former Banbridge Workhouse which now houses the new Health Centre and Polyclinic. These sightings have included a man walking in the grounds near the perimeter fence who then suddenly disappears. On a separate occasion, two people crossed the road in front of another local person one night beside the old hospital and they also suddenly vanished. Local people claim that these are the spirits of the deceased former inmates of the workhouse or of former patients from the hospital which was built on the same site.

Downpatrick Workhouse

The Union Workhouse on the Lisburn Road in Belfast is now the site of the old City Hospital. This workhouse was said to have been haunted. Once there was a cruel warden working here. He was known to have locked up inmates in the Lunatic Asylum Section and beat them until they would die. One such male inmate was chained to the cell floor and later died there. Afterwards, there was an inquest but no explanation could be given as to why the body was covered in bruises.

Apparently, a strange figure dressed in ragged clothes was often seen haunting the workhouse any time a suspicious death in the asylum occurred. Eventually the rules of the workhouse were amended and no more suspicious deaths happened at the hands of the warden.

An image of Banbridge Workhouse

The Butler Ghost of Millisle

Millisle is a village on the Ards Peninsula about three miles south of Donaghadee. Woburn House was the home of the former Lisnevin Training School for Prison Officers and before that a young offender's home called 'The Borstal'. Its original purpose was that of a family summer house. Many claim that the building is haunted by ghosts who walk its halls by night. One story concerns the 'butler ghost'.
The butler had an affair with one of the maids of the house and she became pregnant. Being married and scared of the consequences he became quite desperate and decided to murder her. After the dreadful deed he dragged her body through an underground tunnel beyond the property and threw it off the rocks into the sea. These rocks are named Barkley Rocks; so named after the butler Robert Barkley. Barkley is reported to have returned to the building and hung himself in one of the upstairs rooms. Their ghosts still roam Woburn House.

Burnt Corpse Haunts House in Tullyorior

Years ago in Tullyorior, Annaclone, a young girl of twelve was tragically killed when she fell into an open fire. The house where this happened no longer stands as the family built a new two storey dwelling on the former site. In recent years, there have been strange things going on with the young girl's presence felt and her ghost has been seen several times.

As late as 2007, two members of the family and some friends suddenly heard a loud bang upstairs. They all left the house immediately and ran into the garden.

One girl tripped and fell as she was running out of the house and as the others looked back at her, they noticed someone in the upstairs windows. A face appeared and seemed to smile at them. Everyone saw this face, a sight they would never forget! The face was that of a young girl but it was horrible, almost orange in colour as if badly burnt and with black straggly hair. Her badly burnt hand was also visible as it pulled back the blinds. Her smile was not a welcoming smile, more like an evil smirk.

The girls ran for help and when their uncle searched the house, he could find no trace of the ghost at the window. Three weeks later one of the girls had to go to the bathroom during the night. On her way back to the bedroom, she noticed something standing at the top of the stairs. It was the same ghost! Its face was orange and it had that same eerie smile that she and her friends had noticed before. She ran to her bedroom as fast as she could and was still frightened to leave her bedroom even the next day. This girl has since left home to go to university but still recalls this incident every time she goes home and climbs the stairs. The mother of the house also experienced a strange presence. While she was cleaning her hot press at the top of the stairwell, she felt someone walk past her even though there was no-one else in the house that day. After these incidents the family decided to get their house blessed by the local clergy.

Ardglass Golf Club

The club house of Ardglass Golf Club is one of the oldest club house buildings in the world and dates from the 18th century but the warehouses in the grounds date from 1400 and Horn Castle near the first tee dates from 1377.

Like all very old towns and buildings, Ardglass has its share of ghosts and other strange tales. The ghost of a 'grey lady' has been seen passing through the club house walls where there used to be doors. In the bar, patrons have reported hearing snooker being played but the noise comes from an empty room upstairs which used to be the snooker room. When some renovations were being carried out in 1927, workmen unearthed the skeletal remains of a young child in the wall cavity within the club house. An inquest had to be carried out before its burial in one of the local graveyards.

Ardglass Golf Club

Ghostly Priest in Annaclone Chapel

It was an extremely still night when all of a sudden there was a huge gust of wind that seemed to come out of nowhere. Canon McCorry was the parish priest of Annaclone at the time and Fr. Devlin was the curate. Both priests heard wrecking outside the chapel and they were puzzled by the noise. Fr. Devlin offered to go outside but Canon McCorry was not happy to let him proceed out on his own. This was the 1920s, there was a lot of trouble at that time and he was worried that it may have been Black and Tan soldiers so it was best to stay indoors.

However, Fr. Devlin decided to go out anyway and ignored the Canon's advice. He felt as if something was drawing him out of the parochial house. Walking towards the sacristy door he noticed that there as a priest standing inside wearing his vestments and ready to say Mass. He spoke to Fr. Devlin and asked him if there was anyone here to serve and answer the Mass?

The mysterious priest told him that he had been paid to say mass for a soul in purgatory and he had forgotten to do so and that was why he came back. Fr. Devlin was confused but agreed to help with the Mass; just as it finished there was another large gust of wind and the mysterious priest appeared to fly away like a dove. Fr. Devlin never really got over this event in the chapel and he died a young man.

The Ghost of Old Ballyroney Chapel

Hundreds of years ago there used to be a Catholic Chapel in Drumballyroney near the seat of the Magennis Clan and where they used to worship and were buried. The church itself would have dated from the 14th century but it was destroyed by Cromwellian Forces in the 17th century. A replacement church was later built on the site and it still stands today. However, it is claimed that it is built over the Magennis's graves and the former memorial stone was broken up and thrown into a ditch.

People claim that on the anniversary of the death of the Chief Magennis, a noise can be heard inside the church coming from beneath the floor. It sounds as if someone is trying to get out. In the 1800s a local minister heard the knocking sound and thought perhaps it was an animal trapped under the floor. He prised open some of the floor boards to investigate and it is said that the ghost of Magennis suddenly appeared in front of him.

He was so frightened that he ran home. However, when he had calmed down, the next day, he brought two men with him to help him find out more. They searched further and discovered skulls and other human bones beneath the floor. They then sealed the floor. The same minister who used to have black hair turned very white shortly afterwards. Meanwhile the distant knocking can still be heard!

Raholp Funeral Ghost

Some two hundred years ago, a man from Raholp, outside Downpatrick died. His family held the usual wake and funeral for him although they were not sorry to see him go as he was a tyrant and had made their lives miserable. As the funeral cortege was leaving his former home on its way to the nearby cemetery, the mourners were shocked and dismayed to see the face of the deceased staring out from one of his windows. It appeared that he was laughing at his own funeral!

The mourners were thrown into confusion and scattered and the funeral horses bolted in fright. Eventually, the funeral started out again but the horses would not budge no matter how hard the undertaker tried. It was suggested that he use a donkey to pull the hearse. This worked and his remains reached the cemetery. However, the deceased was buried in an unmarked grave.

His wife and daughter lived contentedly for a number of years until one night while saying their prayers, they heard an unearthly laugh coming from the walls of the house. Suddenly the ghost of the old man appeared and he proceeded to laugh at them until dawn the next day. The same horrible haunting continued each night until they decided to call in the local priest to help them. The priest was overwhelmed by his task and felt he needed to get some help and indeed several priests attended the exorcism. They all noticed a strange unearthly atmosphere when they entered the house.

The exorcism began with the priests calling out for the old man to appear. After the third attempt, the spectre revealed itself. The priests placed a bottle on the floor and then continued by saying a number of prayers and sprinkling the room with holy water. Finally the spirit was forced into the bottle but it let out one last mocking screech. The bottle was quickly sealed and hidden beneath an old mill wheel where it was destined to remain undisturbed for one hundred years.

That period of time has now passed and some local people claim to have seen the ghost of the old man as he searches for his former home.

Raholp Funeral Ghost

Haunted House in Lenaderg

In the 1950s, a young boy was visiting his relatives who were tenants of a large house in Lenaderg. Evening was approaching and the boy was asked by his aunt to go into the back garden and bring in all her washing from the clothes line. As he was doing this, the form of a white figure appeared in front of him and seemed to be coming across the lawn in his direction. The boy was so frightened that he dropped the washing and ran inside. Once inside, he was so afraid that he did not even mention it to his aunt.

Years passed and the boy lost touch with his relatives. However he did meet up with them when he was much older. The conversation came round to the old house in Lenaderg and he decided to ask his aunt if she had ever experienced any paranormal activity there. She replied that she had indeed. It turned out that she had met the same white figure but did not hang around too long and gave up her tenancy very shortly afterwards. The family never found out who or what the figure was.

The Ghost of Killyleagh Mill

This story comes from the end of the last century and involves the local master of the mill who had not been at work as he was ill for some time. A fellow worker claimed to have said hello to the master one morning as he saw him standing at one of the store doors in the mill. He thought it strange that the master did not reply, however, it was only when he recounted this event to another colleague that he started to wonder. When he commented that his master was looking a lot better, his colleague started laughing. He was then told that the master had actually died earlier that day. It was his master's spirit that he had seen and this made him shiver!

Spirits Seen Leaving Buildings in Leitrim

There is a house located beside the old hall in Leitrim. After its occupant, an old lady had died, the house was being renovated and two local men saw the dead woman leaving the dwelling. She was seen walking through the front door. One of the workmen asked the other if he had seen her and he replied, *"Yeah, I did, sure I followed her as she was leaving through the front door!"* Both men knew the old woman and that she was indeed deceased. Although scared by their encounter, the men continued with their work.

A similar incident occurred at Leitrim Post Office when it was being demolished. The digger driver was taking down part of a wall when a small woman walked out of the building. He was so frightened at this sight that he jumped out of his digger and ran away! He did not know the woman but she may have been someone who used to live in the house.

Haunted House near Portaferry

Tara Fort is situated just outside Portaferry and below its southern slope is situated an old house known locally as Widecombe's. Jonathan Widecombe was the local coastguard. A Captain Savage once lived in the house and in 1866 his sailing ship 'The Express' was lost at sea as it journeyed from Portland Oregon to San Francisco. On board were also approximately five crewmen from Portaferry. Captain Savage is still said to haunt his former home. Even on a dry day, the roadway between the house and the trees becomes very wet and local people claim that this is the drowned captain making his way back home. Others have heard the sound of clinking coins as the captain counts all his savings.

In the late 1920s, another sea captain was walking past the

house one night and noticed a family sitting having a meal in the front room. As he had been away for some time, he asked who was now living in Widecombe's house. He was very taken aback when he was told that the house had been empty for some time. Others who stayed in the same house would complain about the phantom diners. One lady was wakened from her sleep by the sound of someone laying plates on the table and when she investigated discovered that it had been set for a meal. Later on that night she was wakened again by more clattering of dishes and then observed that the table had been cleared. Eventually, all the noise at night became too much and the lady moved out. The same house has also been used as a holiday home more recently. For one family, the two youngest children adamantly refused to sleep in their room after the first night of their stay. They complained that the room felt 'funny', freezing cold and there was too much noise.

The Mystery of the Great Bell of Inch Abbey

Inch Abbey is a late twelfth century Cistercian Abbey situated on the banks of the Quoile River.

A great bell once hung in the Abbey and was used by the monks to warn the simple village people nearby of death and destruction as rampaging Vikings swept across County Down. However, the Abbey itself was later destroyed and its bell disappeared. It is said that the monks took it out on the river and let it sink to be buried in the deep river mud to prevent its capture.

The traditional poem 'The Burial of the Bell' tells how the monks rowed away from the Abbey and when they plunged the mighty bell into the water, they recited these words, *"No hand shall desecrate it, no tyrant stamp it slave"*.

The bell has never been found despite many searches of the

river. It is said that the bell still sounds occasional warnings from its watery grave.

When Downpatrick or County Down is threatened by invaders or if some evil force descends on the area, it is rumoured that the Great Bell of Inch will peal again as a warning to its population.

A local lady used to regularly see a boat with three men in it out on the Quoile River. Two of the men were rowing and the third was working with a rope at the stern. When she mentioned this to her husband who had been with her at all of these so called sightings, he admitted that he had never seen the boat and neither had anyone else. The lady who had psychic powers, remembered that the men appeared to be wearing brown sweaters but now believes that she had witnessed the spirits of the Abbey monks, dressed in their brown habits as they buried the Great Bell.

The Blue Lady of Killyleagh Castle

In Killyleagh several local people would swear that they have seen the Blue Lady as she walks along the castle parapets and glances over the town. She is described as wearing old-style clothing.

Few of these people would repeat their story as they feel that they would be laughed at. Killyleagh Castle is one of Ireland's oldest continually inhabited residences. The Blue Lady is said to be the restless spirit of one of the Hamilton family who lived here in the seventeenth century. Lady Alice decided to burn all her husband's wills and forced him to change them in her favour. She died in 1677 and her spirit is said to haunt the castle. Today many people will not walk past the castle late at night on their own and few will remain inside the castle on their own.

Killyleagh Castle

The Haunted Gates of Finnebrogue

Finnebrogue House lies close to Inch Abbey and it is said that the stones from the Abbey were used when building the entrance pillars. When workmen hung the huge ornamental gates, the next day the gates would be found lying flat on the ground yet the gates brackets remained untouched. Each time the gates were hung, they were found on the ground the following day.

It was decided to post men at the gates in order to unravel the mystery. The men waited patiently as darkness fell and then all of a sudden, they saw the gates lifting all by themselves and falling on the ground nearby. There was no sign of anyone nearby. The men were clearly frightened and ran off to the house. Even without the gates, horses refused to pass through the pillars and they had to be dragged through them blindfolded. Many visitors had to dismount or leave their coaches and walk to the house.

Eventually new pillars were built at a new entrance and driveway and the gates were able to be hung undisturbed. The haunted pillars of Finnebrogue became overgrown and remain so to this day. No explanation has ever been given for this strange story.

The Haunted Gates of Finnebrogue

Ballela Hand

In the early 1980s, a child called Martin and his family lived with his grandparents in the townland of Garvaghy. His granddad and Martin never really got on. Some years after the grandfather died, Martin and his parents moved back to Banbridge. In those days, families had to hand down the beds to each other and Martin was given his grandfather's bed.

A year or so passed and Martin was sleeping one night when all of a sudden he was awakened. The bed was up against the wall and when he managed to look around, he saw a red hand coming up the side of the bed. Martin tried to scream but

he could not breathe nor make a sound as he was so afraid.
Eventually he managed to scream and shouted for his parents.
The hand disappeared again down the side of the bed.

The family then threw the bed outside and set fire to it. They
also got the local priest to bless their house. To this day,
Martin who is in his forties still sleeps with the light on at
night and he will not put his bed near the wall. He believes
that the incident was real and it did have a big effect on his
life.

The White Lady of Greencastle

During the 16th century, H. Rupert de Burgh was the Lord
of Greencastle. On a trip to Rome, Italy, the young lord fell
in love with a beautiful girl called Jeanne Pearlin. Although
she at first rejected all his advances, she eventually agreed to
marry him. The young couple were very happy at first but
then de Burgh started to tire of his new fiancée. Rather than
break off their engagement, he decided to take the cowardly
decision to return home. He claimed that he had urgent
family business to attend to and needed to go home urgently.

The young Jeanne was dismayed and pleaded for him to take
her with him. Just as his carriage was leaving, she opened
its door and tried to enter. De Burgh pushed her back and
demanded that the driver proceed as quickly as possible;
Jeanne fell back and was run over by one of the wheels and
was so badly injured that she died. De Burgh never looked
back and fled back to Greencastle as quickly as possible.

It was quite late when he eventually arrived home and just as
his carriage reached the gates to the castle, the horses stopped
and refused to move any further.

De Burgh looked out to see what the delay was and was
horrified by the sight of a white gleaming face peering down

at him from the top of the stone archway which stood over the entrance gates. A hand then reached upwards to the face and pointed to its forehead which bore the marks of a ghastly wound. De Burgh looked closer and realised that this face was that of his fiancée Jeanne.

The horses then suddenly bolted forward and as the carriage entered through the gates, he could hear a loud mocking laugh. That night many strange things happened in the castle. Servants could hear doors opening and closing and the sound of tiny feet running along the stone corridors. These hauntings continued for a long time. De Burgh did marry again but he and his new wife died soon after and the castle passed into other hands.

Many years later, one of the maids who worked in the castle got engaged to a local man. One night they agreed to meet in the castle grounds after their work was done for the day. Her fiancé arrived first and waited for her but she was delayed and soon it got very late. Midnight arrived and he could see the figure of a young woman coming towards him. Thinking this was his fiancée, he ran to meet her and threw his arms around her. But he only clasped air. The figure appeared to run through him and continued on her journey through the garden. He could not understand what had happened and being curious, he followed. He could not catch up with her but after some time, the path split and it was only then that the figure turned around. It revealed a face that made him recoil in horror!

Her hand pointed up to a gaping wound in her forehead. The figure turned round again and went on with its journey. The young man was frozen to the spot but did manage to return home where he later told his story. This was indeed the ghost of the 'White Lady' once again haunting the old castle.

Lissize's Ghost

Many years ago in the 1700s, a young Lissize girl was unfortunately burnt to death in a house fire. She was so badly burnt that the coffin could not be opened during her wake. At the wake, her family and neighbours took turns to sit near the coffin. As with all Irish wakes, the curtains were pulled and the mirrors were covered in the room where the coffin was laid out.

On one occasion, there were only two ladies sitting with the coffin when a strong wind blew into the room and forced the cover off one of the mirrors and to their horror, they saw the girl's badly disfigured reflection. Somehow they managed to cover the mirror once again but they were so traumatised that they could not bring themselves to tell the young girl's family what had happened.

They left the house as quickly as they could and vowed never to attend another wake. The ladies later moved to Belfast. This story was told by one of their granddaughters who made the journey back to Lissize and visited the site of the house where the incident occurred.

The Ghost of Castlewellan Castle

Nearly every old castle has a ghost story linked to it and Castlewellan Castle is no exception. This story originated from staff who used to work in the castle in the early 1900s.

It was a dark winter's night when one of the servants heard a loud noise coming from one of the upstairs rooms. When he went to investigate, he saw a large figure dressed in white emerging very fast from one of the bedrooms. It seemed to the servant that the figure was trying to escape from something or someone and was very frightened. The servant was also frightened by what he had seen and ran to his own room where he locked himself in for the rest of the night.

Over the years the same servant claimed to have seen the figure again coming out of different rooms at night. He was convinced that the spectre was one of the Annesley family who used to live in the castle. When he mentioned seeing the ghost to the then current Lord Annesley, he was laughed at. His master told the servant to go to bed earlier rather than creeping around the castle late at night.

Castlewellan Castle

Country House Ghost

This story involved a man who was visiting an old friend at his country house in County Down. His friend had recently remarried after the death of his first wife.

As he slept in his bedroom on that first night of his visit, he was wakened by a figure of a woman opening his bedroom door. She seemed to be distressed so he asked her what was wrong. There was no reply and as he tried to light a nearby candle, the figure disappeared. He thought he had been dreaming and two hours later he was still unable to get back to sleep when he noticed the door to his room open again. In walked the female figure once again without making any sound.

He managed to get a better look and recognised her from a portrait that was hanging in the dining room downstairs. Tears were pouring down the woman's face as she went over to the window to look outside. The visitor could then hear the sound of a child crying. Once again as soon as the visitor spoke, the figure vanished.

The next morning, the visitor told his host about what had happened to him during the night. It was explained that the lady he had seen was in fact his first wife who had died of a broken heart flowing the death of their only child. The child had fallen from the window in that same bedroom. His wife became very ill afterwards due to her grief and died from a broken heart. She continued to haunt this room and her ghost had also been seen by several other people.

The Phantom Undertaker near Katesbridge

Some years ago Mick went to help his friend Paddy in Aughnacloy, near Katesbridge and had agreed to stay with him all day to help him as there was a lot of work to do on the farm. Little did Mick know that he would remember this visit for the rest of his life. Mick cycled from Banbridge out to Aughnacloy and was welcomed by Paddy who had eagerly been awaiting his arrival.

The two men spent most of the day sorting out cattle and moving them into different fields and darkness soon fell. They had dinner and Mick was asked to stay over as he did not have any lights on his bicycle to light up his return journey home and his friend needed him to work for him the next day as well. Although Mick had heard stories about his friend's house being haunted, he did not want to let him down. Mick had heard that other workers and visitors would have slept in the barn and not in the house. But Mick agreed to stay overnight and was given a room at the back of the house.

As he entered the room he noticed that the battery lamp in the corner continued to flicker on and off. He crept into bed and almost immediately he heard what sounded like a car pulling up outside the gate. Mick shouted at Paddy, *"There is someone outside!"* but Paddy replied, *"Stop talking nonsense and go back to sleep!"* Mick listened intently and heard the house door open and someone entering.

Once again he shouted to his friend but Mick was told that it was his imagination. Then Mick heard footsteps on the stairs and he began to be very afraid. The footsteps got louder and louder and then his room door opened. He could just about make out a dark shadow come towards his bed. It had the appearance of a very tall person. As the light continued to flicker on and off he could see that the person wore a large bowler hat. The next thing, Mick could feel hands around his body as if he was being lifted out of the bed.

Although he tried hard, he could not shout out for help as he was so frightened and had completely lost his voice. He tried to pull the bedclothes over his head but the spirit had a strong hold on him and he could not move. Suddenly there was a white light which took the shape of someone's body being lifted up from the bed. The dark figure appeared to carry it in his arms and then out of the room.

Mick was terrified and ran into Paddy's room shouting *"What the hell did you put me in that room for if you knew it was haunted?"* Paddy replied, *"How do you think I feel for I have to live here!"*

His friend then went on to explain that a woman had been murdered in Mick's room years ago and an undertaker kept coming back to take her body away.

The Phantom Undertaker near Katesbridge

Downpatrick Liver Story

In the early 19th century this story emerged from Downpatrick. A local man named George managed to get a new job with a wealthy family in the town. After his first week, his new employer was invited by his boss to have dinner with him and meet his family. George was delighted and said he was honoured to be asked to dinner and enquired as to what type of food his employer preferred. He replied that he loved liver.

When George came home, he asked his wife to purchase some liver and she in turn told her eldest son to carry out the task and go to the local butcher. The son was studying to be a doctor. He went out to purchase the liver but on his way he met some of his friends and he spent a lot of time with them gossiping and catching up on the local news. At last he remembered to go to the butchers but it was closed for the day. Knowing that the liver was a very important present for his father, he started to panic. Where would he get liver at this late hour?

He suddenly remembered that one of his relations had been buried the day before so he decided to dig up the body and remove its liver. His father duly went to dinner at his employer's house and they all enjoyed the delicious meal. Everyone commented how good the liver tasted.

The son thought that he had got away with his liver deception and later on that night he retired to bed. However, as he lay trying to sleep, he heard footsteps on the stairs. His bedroom door suddenly opened and there stood the figure of his relation from whom he had removed the liver earlier. *"Where is my liver?"* the angry figure demanded.

The next morning, as George's family sat down for breakfast, there was no sign of his son and he did not respond to their calls. A dreadful sight met their eyes as they went upstairs to his bedroom. The son was found dead in his bed but the strangest thing was that his liver had been removed!

Spirits at Large, Kilcoo

Micky McBride's uncle was seriously ill and dying but he decided he would be able to go to visit his girlfriend who lived in Leitrim. On his return in the early morning and as he walked along the lane which approached his uncle's house, he noticed a man leaning over the gate close to the house. As he got closer, he recognised the figure as that of his uncle. The figure then moved and entered the house by the front door. Micky continued to the house and as he walked in, he learned that his uncle had just passed away!

Spring in the Step, Kilcoo

Jamesie was crippled with pains and very stooped over. When he died his body had to be tied down to the bed with ropes so that it would appear his body was straight as he was laid out. As was the custom many years ago, during the wake, men and women would sit in separate rooms and would take it in turns to sit with the corpse. The men went to get refreshments so the ladies then took their turn in the wake room.

One wise head decided to play a trick on the women. He crawled under the bed and taking a tobacco knife from his pocket, he cut the ropes just as the women were settling down. Immediately the corpse jolted up! The women were horrified and screamed as they fled the room making a very quick exit!

Headless Ghost of Castlereagh

This story is based on a murder which occurred in County Down around 1899. The owner of a house came across an intruder to his property and realising that a robbery was taking place, he started to struggle with the burglar. Unfortunately, during the struggle, the owner was killed and he actually had his head cut off.

The house lay vacant for many years but eventually the family decided to sell it hoping that no-one would remember the dreadful murder that had taken place in it all those years earlier. The estate agents advertised the sale outside of the area. The advertisement was noticed by a gentleman who had returned from America with a small fortune and who was keen to settle down in his native land once again.

A viewing was arranged and the estate agent met up with the potential buyer a few weeks later. As they were viewing the house and going around the downstairs rooms, a noise was heard from upstairs. The American gentleman joked that someone was trying to stop him from buying the house. Then a voice was heard again from upstairs saying, *"I am coming down!"*

Again the American joked that someone was going to a lot of trouble to put him off buying this house. Just as they were approaching the stairs, what appeared to be a head rolled down from the top landing! The two men ran out of the house as quickly as possible with the estate agent the first to escape. The American turned around and saw that the 'head' was now at shoulder height.

A voice was heard once again *"Is it the price that is putting you off buying the house?"*

You can imagine that particular sale did not go through and from then on, the house was never sold and was left to fall into ruins.

The Bronte Ghosts

Just south of Rathfriland on the Banbridge Road lies Drumballyroney Church and the Bronte School. The buildings are said to be haunted by the Bronte family. Patrick Bronte was at one time the minister and he also taught in the school. His spirit is said to roam the church and the adjacent graveyard at night.

A team of ghost searchers visited the church in November 2009 and they had some very interesting findings. During their investigation they heard footsteps walking up the aisle of the Church and a number of them saw a figure walking around the graveyard. A photographer also took some photos inside the church and there seemed to be strange light anomalies in the photographs. While inside the school the investigators recording equipment picked up a child saying that her name was Molly and that she attended the school. The ghost also stated that there were 6 pupils at the school. It did not seem that the ghost was annoyed with the investigators for being there but rather that she wanted to communicate with them.

Another person made contact with the investigators. He said the words *"Bronte School"* and added that his name was Patrick. Could this be the ghost of Patrick Bronte? During the recording you can clearly hear these words being spoken. Throughout the night the whole team were extremely cold and they could feel a presence.

Drumballyroney Church near Rathfriland

Whilst in the church something or someone tried to take the camera off the cameraman and their recording device was knocked over. On the video you can see a wire on the woman's headphones being tugged. The investigators also heard a large bang and footsteps and a few knocks towards the back of the church. Their camera went strangely out of focus and eventually they had to stop recording. Many of them believed that it may have been the infamous Squire Hawkins letting his presence be known. (See Chapter 6)

Strange Tale of Mrs Butler

The story concerns the bi-location of an Irish lady called Mrs Butler who started to have dreams about a beautiful house. She could vividly describe the house with its conservatory and manicured garden. In her dreams she visited this house many times and she felt very happy and content with herself as she walked around the rooms. Her husband and family used to joke about her 'nightly visits'.

Some years later, the family had to re-locate to England and started to look for houses. They went to view a house in Hampshire and immediately as Mrs Butler approached it, she recognised it from her dreams and mentioned this to her husband. When the housekeeper offered to show them around, Mrs Butler asked if she could do the showing. She was able to locate the rooms successfully until she came across a door that she did not remember. *"That door is not in my house"* she said and the housekeeper replied that the door had only been installed several weeks prior.

The Butlers decided to buy the house and were surprised how cheap it was but no-one could give them a suitable explanation. After they had signed the deeds they once again asked why the house was so cheap. The estate agent, who had initially been quite distressed to see Mrs Butler, began to explain.

"There can be no harm in telling you now that this house was known to be haunted: but you, Madam, need be under no apprehensions for you are yourself the ghost!"

The implication seemed to be that Mrs Butler had been haunting the house while she believed herself to be dreaming of it! The poor estate agent had seen her ghost and immediately recognised her when enquiries were made to view the house.

Chapter 2
Ghosts & Transport

Introduction

Ghosts are not just confined to stately homes and castles. There are many tales related to trains, cars, horse and carriages and boats. One story exists of a ghostly ship which is said to forewarn those who see it of an impending disaster. The 'Flying Dutchman' is probably the most famous of such ghost or phantom ships. Its legend tells of a ship sailing around the Cape of Good Hope during a very bad storm. The captain would not let the crew take the ship in to one of the safe harbours in the area as he insisted the ship would be safe and not sink. As the crew prayed for their safety, a glowing form appeared on the deck of the ship and the crew believed it was the image of Christ. The captain however dismissed the apparition and boasted that even God could not sink his ship! The spirit then placed a curse on the ship and doomed it to sail the seas forever and to bring bad luck to any sailor who might see it.

The Girl from Ballymullan

Most ghost stories concerning children are centred around a tragic event and the following is no exception. People also believe that animals, particularly horses see things which are not visible to the human eye. There are many stories about horses that refuse to pass a certain place or become so frightened that they bolt and run away. Some say that if you looked into the horses eyes at that time, one will see a reflection of what it actually saw.

Ballymullan is a small townland lying between Crawfordsburn and Helen's Bay. In the late 1920s, a man was driving his horse and cart along the road when he noticed a very young and very pale girl standing at the side of the road. His horse became very unsettled as they passed the girl, however, she herself paid no attention to the horse and cart and appeared to stare right through them. Curious, the man stopped to ask if the girl was alright but when he looked back, she had disappeared. He dismounted and searched all around but to no avail and then his horse suddenly bolted and galloped along the road. Eventually he caught up with the horse and saw that it was very distressed. He walked alongside it for some distance to calm it down.

Reaching a small cottage he asked for some water for the horse and then told the occupants the story of the little girl. Immediately, they were able to tell him of a tragedy that occurred along that particular stretch of road. Years previously, a young girl had fallen from a lorry and had been killed. Other people had also told of seeing her ghost standing at the roadside.

Dundrum Taxi Ghost

This strange tale comes from the 1980s in the village of Dundrum, near Newcastle. A Dundrum resident frequented his local pub each and every Friday night. One particular night, he stayed at the pub longer than usual and had drunk more alcohol as well. He came out of the pub around 1.30am. He saw a taxi across the street and decided to go home in it. When he looked inside the taxi, he did not see any driver. However, the taxi was not locked and he got inside to wait for its driver.

All of a sudden, the taxi started to move forward! He then thought he saw a dark shadow in the driver's seat. Paralysed with fear, the man just sat in the back seat. Nearly two miles later, the taxi slowed down and stopped outside a garage. Seeing this as a chance to escape, he opened the door and stumbled out of the taxi running away as fast as he could. At a safe distance, he stopped and looked back.

He could not believe his eyes! The taxi driver was actually

pushing his broken down car from behind. There was no ghostly driver after all and the taxi had been pushed the whole way from the main street in Dundrum! The man felt so stupid and vowed never again to consume so much alcohol.

Dundrum Taxi Ghost

The Mystery of the Disappearing Cyclist

This 1960s story came from the Down Recorder and involves the Rathmullan area. It was told by three delivery men who were returning home from doing their rounds.

As they were passing the bend at Rathmullan Church, a cyclist suddenly appeared on the road in front of their van. Despite applying the brakes as hard and as quickly as possible, the driver could not avoid hitting the cyclist. He and his bicycle disappeared under the van. The occupants jumped out and ran back down the darkened road and searched for the injured party but there was no sign of him or his bicycle. The driver reversed back and put the van lights on fully to help in the search but no trace was found. As they talked about the strange disappearance, they also remembered that there was no noise and no bump as they collided with the cyclist. They all could describe the cyclist and what he was wearing – a large grey overcoat with the lapels turned up over his face and he wore a flat cap on his head. They then realised that they must have seen a ghost and they became very frightened.

One year later, the same men were on the same stretch of road. The youngest was sitting in the back of the van with the doors open as they made their deliveries. Driving about 40mph, the young man slipped from his seat and fell out of the back of the van and it so happened to be at the exact same spot where the ghostly cyclist had appeared the year before.

The van stopped and they ran back to help the young man as he lay on the road. However, he was able to tell the driver that instead of hurting himself, it felt as if he had landed on a mattress and he was not even bruised or hurt in anyway. The same man maintains that it was the ghostly cyclist who had returned and prevented him from what should have been a very nasty accident indeed.

A1 & Other Roads Ghost Stories

Stories of vanishing travellers have occurred throughout the centuries and while the types of vehicles have changed, the basic sequence of events has remained the same.

The A1 is a major road that runs through County Down and mainly from Newry to Belfast. Over forty years ago, a local man was driving along a stretch of the A1 in the early hours of the morning. The road would have been a single carriageway at that time. Coming round a bend, he noticed a young man standing at the side of the road. He appeared to be a soldier as he was wearing a heavy coat and had a kit bag over his shoulder and looked as if he was waiting for a lift. After passing the soldier, the curious driver looked back in his mirror but there was no sign of the soldier. He stopped his car and looked all around for the soldier but no-one was there. What had the driver seen? Was this soldier a vision from the past?

Another story from the A1 involves another driver coming home from his work in Belfast one dark winter's evening. Suddenly he saw a young woman in her early twenties looking for a lift. He noticed that although she wore a coat, she did not have any bag or gloves. Concerned about her well-being, and being a father himself, he stopped to give the woman a lift. Not a word was spoken by her even when the driver asked where she was going. Some distance on, the driver felt an icy chill and he turned to look at his passenger only to discover that she had vanished!

He was so startled that he slammed on his brakes and then managed to stumble outside. But there was no-one there! He even checked the passenger door but was satisfied that there was no way that the woman could have got out of his car without him noticing. Eventually, he calmed down and managed to drive further and he went to the nearest police station where he reported his tale of the Phantom Hitch Hiker.

Another similar story involves the Comber to Newtownards Dual Carriageway. A driver noticed a blonde haired girl standing at the side of this main road. As this was somewhat unusual along such a busy dual carriage way, the driver looked back at her in his mirror but there was no sign of her. He pulled in and got out of the car for a closer look and could not see her anywhere. He was very puzzled as there was no clear exit off the road at this particular spot.

The White Lady of the Tullyrain Road, Banbridge

It was late September in 2011 when a woman and her daughter were travelling to Waringstown on the Banbridge Road. The time was between 8.30pm and 9pm and it was starting to get dark. They suddenly noticed a girl dressed in white walking along the grass verge. They both thought that this was very strange as she was very well dressed in a long white gown. She was very pretty with blonde curly hair and a round face. On her feet, she wore small ballet pumps and even though the verge was wet and mucky, her shoes were clean as if she was just floating along and not actually touching the ground.

As they drove past the girl, she turned around and looking at the passenger she smiled. The driver of the car did not observe this but her passenger told the driver to turn around immediately. There was something very strange about the girl and she wanted to get a closer look. There was however a car behind theirs and it was impossible to turn around in the road. The girl seemed to have a white glow around her and both mother and daughter were convinced that she was not human. By the time they got back to that spot again, the figure had disappeared.

Eventually some local people heard the ladies' story and they were able to provide some more information. Decades previously a young woman would have walked that particular stretch of road every day. Others have met the woman as she walks this road and it is believed that this is the spirit of the woman who died many years ago and that she is re-enacting what she did in her youth.

The White Lady of the Tullyrain Road, Banbridge

Carlingford Lough Ghost Ship

Some true events are far stranger that anything that could be dreamed up by even the most skilled fiction writer. Such is the case as happened in April 1959 on the lough coast. Two Scottish cyclists on a camping holiday had set up camp on a quiet river delta a few yards from the shore. As it was late and fairly dark, they concentrated on erecting their tent and cooking their evening meal. They never got a chance to study their surroundings and tired from the long day in the saddle, they quickly fell asleep.

At around 3 am, they were awakened by something and peering nervously out of their tent, an astonishing sight met their eyes. Docked on the river bank was an ancient three masted sailing ship of the type used on long sea voyages many years ago. The gang plank was lowered and they could see human figures embarking, some carrying bags or cases while others seemed to have belongings wrapped up in little cloth bundles.

This carried on for more than fifteen minutes until a dark cloud obscured the moon and everything turned into darkness. The cyclists retreated back into their tent knowing daybreak was only a couple of hours away and they would then try and wish bon voyage to some of those on board the ship.

However, a thick fog had descended over the land and sea the next morning and they would have to wait a little longer to make their acquaintance with the ship and its passengers. But as the fog lifted, the ship was nowhere to be seen and closer investigation showed that in fact no ship could ever have possibly negotiated into what remained of a very old and rotten wooden wharf. The inlet was completely silted up and so badly that it was doubtful if even a rowing boat could have navigated its way in.

Carlingford Lough

All the cyclists could do was to pack up their tent and move on hoping to meet someone locally who might be able to throw some light on their experience the night before. They did not have to wait long as they came across and old farmer who was using real horse power to plough one of his fields. The pair excitedly approached him and told him their story. But he really surprised them by telling them to, *"Stop your story right there!"* The farmer then related what had happened as if he had been there himself. He continued, *"I have often heard old folk talk about this phenomenon but I never seen it myself."*

Apparently the legend states that one hundred and fifty years or so before, a bad illness or as we would describe now as an epidemic had ravished the entire area. Many old people were unable to withstand it and died. The younger people were now left homeless as the landlords had repossessed the houses previously tenanted by the older folk. They were forced to sell whatever they had to try and get the few pennies needed to move away from the area.

A rather cantankerous sea captain appeared on the scene and offered passage on his ship for the 'right money'. He insisted on as many people as possible be carried as of course the more paying passengers, the more money he pocketed.

The legend also describes bad fogs around that time and the ship was believed to have left at night and possibly in one of the fogs. Whatever the truth was, the ship and its passengers were never heard from again. Did the captain return in spirit with his ship in the hope of finally getting his passengers to their destination? No-one really knows!

The Portaferry Ferryboat Ghost

In 1836, the 'Lady of the Lake' was the name given to the first steam powered ferry boat which operated across Strangford

Lough between Portaferry and Strangford. Among her first passengers were a newly married couple who were setting off on their honeymoon.

In 1838, one very stormy October evening, the lough itself was very rough but the ferry made its journey across. The stormy sea tossed the ferry and its passengers decided to shelter in the passenger cabin. One of these making the crossing to Portaferry was called McHenry and unfortunately he was the worse for drink. There were two doors leading off the deck, one to the cabin and the other to the gearing and the paddle wheel. As the boat pitched and rolled in the tide, poor McHenry lost his balance and as he slipped on the wet deck, he was flung headfirst into the gearing for the paddlewheel and was instantly killed.

His body was eventually brought ashore and taken into one of the nearby cottages. Someone went to inform his family but as it was such a bad night, his family did not arrive until the next morning to take his body home.

Some years later, a sailor and his wife occupied the cottage where McHenry's body had been taken to. The sailor was often away and his wife was left on her own for long periods of time. On another wet and windy night, one of the sailor's friends knocked at the cottage door and asked for shelter for himself and his donkey. A bed was made up for the man in the downstairs room and the donkey was sheltered in the yard at the back of the cottage. The next morning, she asked her visitor if he had slept well. He replied that he had endured a dreadful night.

Somewhat surprised, the woman asked why. She was told that although the bed was very comfortable and the room was warm, he had been wakened by the noise of someone at the bottom of the stairs. The visitor managed to sit up and light a candle and then saw the ghost of a man so severely mutilated and covered in blood that he was unable to identify him at first. The ghost was trying to climb the stairs but appeared to be very drunk and kept falling back and cursing as he did so. When he called out sharply from his bed, the bloody ghost disappeared. Immediately the sailor's wife who had never heard the story of McHenry and had never witnessed any ghostly sightings, left the cottage. She ran to the local priest and insisted that her home be blessed and rid of this spectre forever.

Ghostly Sightings On Carlingford Lough

The strangest of true stories can be absolutely terrifying for those who bear witness to them. Such was the case of two fishermen in an old wooden rowing boat on Carlingford Lough between Counties Down and Louth just south of Greencastle and Greenore in the spring of 1905. Just as they did every day for over twenty two years, they rowed out to their favourite fishing ground which experience had taught them provided the best chance of landing the shoals of herring to make their living. The day began like any other but the longed for hope of a prize catch did not materialise and as dusk approached they decided to make their way home with only a meagre catch.

They were suddenly alerted to thundering, beating noises in the water some way behind their boat. They soon picked out the astonishing sight of about twenty frightened horses swimming for their lives towards them. Shouting and yelling in panic, the men tried to scare the horses away from their boat. They feared that they were going to be swamped. However, it was no use and soon the petrified animals were almost on top of them.

They both lay down flat in the bottom of their boat amid the few fish they had caught and watched as the spectre of the ghostly animals seemingly passed straight through their boat and then literally disappeared. When the fishermen emerged to look around in the fading light, there was nothing to see or hear.

Back on land, they decided nervously to ask around if anyone had ever experienced the same strange event which had befell them. However, no one had ever heard of such a sighting and as they feared, the fishermen began to become the butt of many jokes. They were often asked what part they had played in the 'Aquatic Grand National'.

A few months passed and the County Down men were once again out herring fishing. They noticed a storm brewing and decided to shelter in a little bay not far from King John's Castle in Carlingford. They decided to pass away a few hours in a local hostelry while the storm passed. They fell into the company of an old man and related their strange story to him.

He did not seem at all surprised and shaking his head, he told them it had been a very long time since anyone had reported the sighting of the unfortunate horses. The men were relieved that at long last someone believed their story and could now offer them an explanation.

The legendary story dates back hundreds of years to when a ship carrying horses to the then garrison town of Carlingford had been caught up in a ferocious storm. The crew decided to save themselves and the ship by forcefully dumping the unfortunate and terrified animals over the side. Even above the noise of the storm, the poor horses could be heard neighing and screaming in terror as they attempted to swim for their lives.

For many years after the terrible ordeal, the horses were often seen in all weathers and always in twilight still terrified and fighting for their lives somewhere out on Carlingford Lough between the coasts of County Down and County Louth.

Strange lights on the Railway at Annacloy

Counties Down and Armagh used to have much bigger rail networks than nowadays. Only two railway lines exist today; the main line between Dublin and Belfast and the Bangor to Belfast line. Many men were injured or killed carrying out the hard manual work involved in bringing the railway in to County Down. It is said that the spirits of these men are still seen walking along the stretch of track where they spent their last days. Such sightings are claimed to have been observed at Annacloy especially after the nightly 9pm train had passed through the village. The lights would bob up and down along the track and all of a sudden shoot off in to the night sky. Many groups of people would gather on a nearby bridge to see this strange sight.

One story involved the local postman who was out driving his van when he spotted the lights on the road ahead of him. One particular light suddenly appeared right in front of him leaving him no time to stop or swerve past it. Thinking that he had actually hit someone with a torch, he stopped and got out to check but the road was completely clear and there was so sign of anyone or anything. The postman could not understand what had happened.

Experts would now argue that the lights were the result a natural phenomenon. Many railway tracks were constructed across bogs and marshes which gave off a gas known as coal damp. This gas would glow and could be seen on clear moonlight nights. These were also known as 'will o' the wisp' or 'bog lights'. However, no-one can explain why the lights were rarely seen after the trains stopped running and the railway tracks were removed.

The Funeral Outside Newcastle

Strange happenings are nothing new and are not confined to the pages of fantasy or ghost stories. One such actual event was witnessed by a Newry taxi-driver on a lonely road outside Hilltown in the early 1970s.

It was Christmas time and the taxi took a group of party-goers from Newcastle to a hotel in Newry. Having returned to Newcastle in the early hours and then making his way home alone, the taxi-driver was shocked to encounter out of the darkness a group of men dressed in somewhat traditional black sombre suits. They also wore Lincoln type top hats and most bizarre of all, they were carrying a coffin!

The taxi-driver respectfully pulled in to the side of the road and waited until the group had passed, thinking that they were simply moving the remains from one house to another for 'waking' and had decided to do so at night to lessen the possibility of meeting traffic. When he later recounted the story, he also remarked that there was no sound whatsoever from the entourage as they walked on the tarmac road with their strong footwear. The taxi-driver was intrigued by the whole experience and being in Hilltown a few days later, he decided to make enquiries in shops, pubs and even in the local livestock sale yard. No-one had heard a whisper about any such a funeral and there were no reports of any locals having died. He could only continue to wonder.

But this was not to be the end of the mystery because exactly one year later to the day and time and again returning to Newry, he once again met the same funeral party at the same place. This time, he drove straight on hoping that the mirage coming towards him was not real. He need not have worried as the funeral party spirits simply vanished as he motored onwards.

Needless to say in the following years as he ferried his fares at Christmas time, he always returned home by a different route!

Cabra Ghosts

In the 1700s one of the local land owners was taking his children on a journey by horse and carriage. It was a cold November day as the family made their way to a local town. All of a sudden the horse was frightened and it bolted causing the carriage to overturn. Tragically all the children were killed and their father survived but was seriously injured. It is said that on the anniversary of the accident, the children's spirits would be seen at night. Firstly the eldest child would appear, then the middle child and lastly before the night was over, the youngest would also appear.

After ten years or so the father was forced to move to Belfast but the children's spirits would still haunt him. He became a tragic figure, not able to escape the terrible events of that November night. Eventually, he could take no more and he took his own life.

The older people in Cabra would still claim that on a November evening, the whole family can be seen walking the road where the original accident occurred. The father has been seen holding his children's hands.

The Ghostly Horse of Lisnabrague

In the 19th century, William Fivey once lived in Lisnabrague Lodge situated outside Loughbrickland. He was a very wealthy landowner and also had several mills. William was however, a prolific gambler and loved nothing more than to go to the racecourse. He also owned and trained a number of horses himself. Unfortunately, he was gambling most of his wealth away and he soon became in financial straits and quite desperate. He decided to gamble everything on one last fling. He believed that his only way out was for his best horse to win a race and for him to put a good wager on it. He prepared and trained the horse himself and was convinced that it could not lose.

However the horse did not win and Fivey was furious as he now faced financial ruin. He was so disgusted with the horse that after it was taken home, he locked it in its stable without food or water and bricked up the doorway. The poor horse died of starvation.

Fivey was forced to sell all his horses and furniture and to rent out his house so that he could pay his gambling debts. Since then, many people have claimed to have seen a ghostly figure of a horse galloping up the avenue to Lisnabrague Lodge on moonlit nights. Indeed, soldiers who were stationed there during the Second World War also told the same story.

The Ghostly Horse of Lisnabrague

The Phantom Coach of Aghaderg

This story was told by a lady whose father was a clergyman living outside Banbridge in the early 1900s. The family lived in a large house which was reached by a short avenue from the main road. There was a large turning area in the front of the house and stables at the back.

One winter's evening, her father was returning home from visiting one of his sick parishioners. As he drove his own carriage up the avenue he was passed by another carriage going at a very fast speed. When he reached the front of the house, there was nothing there and thinking that the carriage had been taken to the back stables, he went inside. He decided to investigate further and asked his servant who had called at the house. The servant replied that no-one had been at the house that evening.

Thinking that this was very strange, the clergyman then asked his family members who were in the drawing room about the carriage. They were able to confirm that they had heard an earlier carriage drive up the avenue but no-one had called at the house. He was able to describe the carriage as being black, closed up and with lit-lamps at the corners. He was a well-respected man and people were sure that his story was indeed true.

On another occasion, another servant arrived back very late from her day off. She rushed into the kitchen, *"I am so sorry to be late"* she proclaimed *"especially as there were visitors. I suppose they stayed to supper as they were so late going away, for I met their carriage on the avenue."*

The cook told her that there had not been any callers to the house that evening and that she must have seen the 'ghost carriage'. Apparently, this phenomenon was well known among the local people of the area.

Chapter 3

Fairy Tales of County Down

An iconic fairy tree located at the Corbet Lough

Introduction

There are very few places in Ireland that do not have a fairy
story or two and County Down is no exception. Many
such stories involve fairy trees and even the kidnapping
of humans! Some places have a concentration of fairy
stories while others only have an isolated tale. The village
of Rostrevor is an area full of Fairy traditions and it is no
surprise that it has an area called the Fairy Glen some say
because fairies used to live along the river banks. Beside the
Fairy Glen is a house called Fairy Hill.

The Irish word for fairy is sheehogue (sidheog). Fairy people
are also known as daoine sidhe (deenee shee) and the word
banshee means fairy woman. Fairies are generally associated
with being small but they can take on any shape or size that
pleases them. Their main occupations are playing beautiful
music, feasting, fighting and making love. The only working
fairy is the 'leprechaun' or the shoemaker needed to replace
the shoes worn out by all the dancing!

Most people will admit that they do not believe in fairies but
very few will go near a 'fairy fort' after dark or disturb a 'fairy
tree'. A 'fairy fort' is normally found in raths and celtic forts
around the countryside. These were built on good vantage
points with circular fenced stockades and also souterrains
(tunnels) nearby. The souterrains were used for defence
and escape purposes and allegedly so that the fairies could
hide in. The word 'Lis' at the start of a place name normally
identifies such a Celtic fort for example:- Lisnavarragh Fort
outside Scarva. It is over 3000 years old and has 3 distinct
concentric ditches. It lies close to the Black Pig Dyke which
once formed part of the old border between the north and the
south of Ireland. It is reported that lights were often seen at
the dyke at night. These were blamed on either smugglers or
the fairies.

Fairy Trees or Thorns

It is easy to spot a 'fairy tree' or 'fairy thorn' as it is usually a lone hawthorn tree. A wise farmer will plough around a 'fairy tree' and engineers and builders will generally avoid interfering with such trees.

It is very unlucky to destroy a fairy fort or cut down a fairy tree!

Other superstitions concerning fairy trees include the following:-

If you walk 3 times around a fairy ring and do not tell anyone what you are wishing for, the fairies will grant your wish;

• You must not run round a fairy ring, you have to walk;

• You must not push anyone off the ring or the fairies will bring you bad luck;

• You must say a prayer and make the sign of the cross by thrusting your thumb between your fore and middle finger, if you travel through fairy land;

• You must never hang clothes to dry on a fairy thorn; and

• Never break off a branch, even by mistake: it must be re-attached as soon as possible.

These enchanted trees are believed to have unearthly powers and the superstitions come from many years ago. Some say that it started when our ancestors travelled from the Mediterranean to settle in Ireland. Along the way, all they had to eat were figs which grew on the blackthorn tree and it therefore became an important source of food. The travellers believed that their gods lived in the trees and they were considered sacred. This belief continued when they settled in

Ireland even though the trees do not produce any fruit here.

Another claim is that the fairy blackthorn tree does not have any sharp thorns on its branches as opposed to the ordinary blackthorn tree. People are warned to stay away from the fairy blackthorn tree.

A Fairy Tree near Ballyward

Annacloy, Saul & Clough Stories

Several tales have been linked to fairy blackthorn trees in the Annacloy, Saul and Clough areas of County Down.

In the 1970s road improvements were planned for the Annacloy area and this involved the cutting down of a small solitary blackthorn tree to make way for a new road. Local people warned the workmen that it was dangerous to cut down the tree and that all sorts of disasters and misfortune would befall anyone who had a hand in it. Unfortunately these warnings were ignored and soon the diggers and lorries moved in. The next day, the people of the village of Annacloy were dismayed and angry when they heard the sad news as some of them had claimed to have seen fairies at the tree.

So many people gathered around where the tree once stood that the Police from Downpatrick had to come to direct traffic. It was almost like a funeral procession as the tree was taken away and buried a few yards from its original location.

It is claimed that even after its destruction, the tree continued to exert its strange powers! Allegedly one of the work men who cut down the tree died shortly afterwards and another caught a serious leg infection which resulted in him having his leg amputated.

Another strange tale involving a fairy tree comes from the Saul area. Before the start of the Second World War an elderly man from nearby Raholp was out walking one frosty moonlight night. Suddenly he overheard strange music and eventually realised that it was coming from a nearby blackthorn tree standing on its own in a nearby field. He was completely enchanted by the music and found himself walking closer to the tree where he came across a group of strange little people laughing and dancing around the tree. Mesmerised by the sight he continued to watch it until near dawn and as the sun rose in the east and lightened the sky he felt himself getting very tired. Just before he fell asleep, he heard a rooster crow and all the little fairies disappeared.

Several hours later the man awoke and found himself all alone in the field. Cold and wet through, he walked home and went to bed where he remained for a whole week suffering from a chill. This lone blackthorn tree still stands today.

Worshipping the Fairy Thorn, Kilkeel

There is a fairy thorn located on the top of a hill on Leestone Road near Kilkeel which people like to worship and they believe that it brings good luck to the area. One local farmer named Cunningham was very superstitious and after each animal was born on his farm he would have taken it to the fairy thorn. A neighbour of his was the 7th daughter of the 7th daughter and he also got her to visit his house just to touch the animal. The farmer never had an animal die and he felt the fairies were to thank for this.

Another woman who lived across the road from the fairy thorn recalled how she used to play with the fairies when she was a child. She explained how during the summer she would be out in the field with her mother and father as they cut the hay. They were in the field next to the fairy thorn. Her parents would have been using the tractor while the young girl and her friend would have played dolls with the fairies. The woman who is in her 40s now does not remember much about their appearance but she definitely recalls playing with little people. She said that people in the area always had a huge respect for the tree and nothing bad ever happened in her family or to anyone in the locality.

The Whitethorn of the Dancing, Warrenpoint

The whitethorn tree has long been associated with the fairies. Such a tree grows in the centre of a field beyond the mill dam between Warrenpoint to Grinan. It is known as The Fairy Tree, 'The Whitethorn of the Dancing'. Traditionally May-Eve was celebrated there many years ago when the children of the areas danced the "Rinceshee" (Fairy Dance) around the tree and sang The Song of May to celebrate the coming of summer. On that night too, as a protection for the year against un-welcome visitors, rowan berries and branches were placed outside every cottage, as were May flowers (primroses). Even to this day you can see May flowers scattered outside some doorways in Ireland.

It was at such a May-Eve gathering many years ago that the daughter of the landowner on whose land the tree grew, brought her little brother with her to the festivities and sat him at the foot of the tree while the others danced. It was a beautiful clear night, but without warning a magical mist descended over the field enveloping everything. When it cleared the girl ran to the foot of the tree to collect her little brother, but in the intervening time he had changed utterly. He was believed to be a 'changeling' and he soon pined away and died.

The child's father was James McDarragh, and he was very angry with the little people and resolved to cut down the 'Fairy Thorn', but a wee old man came to him in a dream and warned him that if he did cut it that more awful things would happen to him but if he left it alone he would be well rewarded.

So he left the tree alone and a few nights later he had another dream. This dream occurred the next night, and the next night. 'Go to Dublin' the dream said and 'repair the bridge that runs through the capital city and you will make your fortune'. Without telling anyone of his foolishness, he travelled to Dublin by stagecoach and on arrival took up position close to the bridge. No one passed any remarks as he stood watching and waiting for 3 days. As nothing happened, he started to feel foolish again at listening to his dreams and he decided to go home.

As he turned to go a man approached him and said to him, *"I've been watching you for 3 days standing here looking at the bridge, do you mind me asking what you're doing."* "Ah" says

McDarragh, *"You wouldn't believe me even if I told you."* *"Try me"* said the man. McDarragh told him about his dream and even managed to smile when thinking about what he had done.

"Well that's a good one" the man replied *"sure I often dream myself, but pay no heed to dreams. Even last night I dreamt that I should go to a farm in Co. Down, owned by a man called James McDarragh and that I should dig in the ditch beside the road, where I would find a pot full of gold coins. Away home with you my man and put no faith in dreams!"*

McDarragh needed no encouragement, and was soon rushing home, willing the horses to go faster along the track to Newry and back to his farm. He got out a spade and started digging, 2 hours in and the spade struck metal. He bent down and grasped a bronze metal urn. He opened the hinged lid, on which there was writing that he could not decipher, and he found it full of ancient gold coins. He took them home and placed them in a chest below the floor boards of his bedroom. He never wanted again for anything.

Some years later, the urn stood empty on the dresser table, when he heard a knock on the front door. He opened it, only to find a weary traveller standing there looking for shelter. He brought him in to the fire as was the custom of hospitality and offered him food and lodgings. As he ate, a flicker of light from the candle caught the script written on the lid of the urn. The traveller stood up to examine it. *"Do you know what it says!"* asked McDarragh. *"It's a very old Celtic script"* said the traveller, *"It says dig on the other side of the Whitethorn of The Dancing and you will get as much more"* *"What a strange message!"* said the traveller. *"Strange indeed"* said McDarragh, barely able to contain himself.

The following morning the traveller thanked him for his

hospitality and McDarragh placed a few gold coins in his pocket as he left. He went to the fairy thorn and began to dig. Soon, he struck the top of another bronze urn a replica of the one he had already found, with the same number of coins, but with no script on the lid. The dream was as good as its word.

Fairy Thorns in Knockararney, Donaghmore

A local farmer decided to remove some thorns which were growing around a fort on his land. Later on that day his eighteen month old colt dropped dead in one of his fields and his sow produced a litter of pigs. The piglets all soon died and so did the mother. Needless to say, the farmer did not do any more work around the fort from then on.

The Disappearing Teapot in Aughnacloy

In the 1950s, an Annaclone man was helping a farmer in Aughnacloy to plant a field of potatoes. At lunch time, they stopped for tea and sandwiches. They decided to hang the teapot on a branch of a tree so that it would not spill. The tree just happened to be a fairy tree. After drinking the first cup, they went to get the teapot for a second cup. However, the teapot was nowhere to be seen. The men searched all around and even inside the tree but there was no sign of their teapot. They were bewildered as to where it might have gone because they knew exactly where it was placed. Eventually they came to the conclusion that the fairies had obviously taken it.

The following year, when the two men were back in the same field, they found themselves sitting beside the fairy tree once again as they ate their lunch. Low and behold here was the teapot hanging on the exact same branch which they had left it on the year before! As if this was not hard enough to believe, the men found the teapot with the tea still inside and it was even warm to touch.

The farmer recalled that in the same field, there used to be two fairy trees but one day, when he was getting some work done, a digger driver actually pulled one of the trees out of the ground before he could stop him. The next day, the farmer found one of his cows lying dead in that very same field.

Disappearing Teapot in Aughnacloy

The Fairy Tree, Mourne Area

This story is based on one told by Steve Lally in his book 'Down Folk Tales'. The tale is of another fairy tree which stood in a remote part of County Down within the Mourne Mountains. The bachelor farmer who owned the land in which it stood was a very miserable man with no regard for the well-being of others. He had only two loves in his life: his land and his money. He was so mean, he would not spend Christmas and he was so ugly that 'he could turn a sunny

73

Friday afternoon into a miserable Monday morning'. He was known as 'Farmer Willy-Spud-Murphy-O'Horrible'. He hated everyone especially trespassers on his land and he constantly inspected his land looking for such unwelcome visitors. He also hated the fairy tree that grew in one of his best fields. Even though his father and grandfather had warned him never to harm or cut down the sacred tree, he was determined to get rid of it. Looking at the tree he sneered, *"You're the ugliest thing I have ever seen, you grow no fruit and you pay no rent. You'll have to go!"* and so he decided to cut it down. He went back home to fetch an axe and his horse and cart. His horse was called 'Sorrow' and he was kept in a leaky old shed with only scraps of unwanted food to eat.

As the farmer started to cut down the fairy tree, there was a mighty clap of thunder and a flash of lightning. A terrible silence fell over the whole place. Undeterred, the farmer continued to chop down the tree. He filled the cart with firewood and forced the poor horse to drag the ill-gotten bounty back to his farmhouse. That night, the farmer enjoyed a blazing fire and he soon fell asleep. All of a sudden, there was an almighty crash and he got such a fright that his eyes actually popped out of his head. They rolled across the floor, up the walls and finally landed in his pockets. He managed to reach down and put them back in again.

He then was able to see a hideous troll in the room who started to scold him for all his miserable deeds including cutting down his tree. O'Horrible reminded the troll that the tree was on his land and that he could do anything he wanted with it. He angrily told the troll to leave his house. The troll then grabbed the farmer and trailed him outside to the spot where the fairy tree once stood. O' Horrible was surprised to see that the fairy tree had grown back and was completely surrounded by all types of fairy creatures who were singing and dancing around it. When they saw the farmer, they started to dance around him but they were all in a very angry mood. Gradually the farmer was pushed against the tree and then he was squashed into it.

Next morning the farmer and even his horse were nowhere to be seen and gradually the local people came onto his land and knocked his house down. The fairy tree still stands proudly in the field but if one looks closer, once can see a gnarled face in its trunk. The farmer's poor horse, Sorrow, was rescued by the fairies and now runs with the magical horses of 'Tir na Nog' and lives a happy existence away from its previous owner.

O'Horrible however complained so much about his fate that eventually he had to apologise for all his wrong doings and he promised to make amends. The fairies did release him out of the tree eventually and gave him the job of taking care of all the fairy trees in the county. Sometimes he is seen on dark nights especially during Halloween, tending and watering the trees. He appears to be a very happy grateful man.

The Fairy Tree, Mourne Area

The Fairy Thorn

"GET up, our Anna dear, from the weary spinning-wheel;
For your father's on the hill, and your mother is asleep;
Come up above the crags, and we'll dance a highland-reel
Around the fairy thorn on the steep."

At Anna Grace's door 'twas thus the maidens cried,
Three merry maidens fair in kirtles of the green;
And Anna laid the rock and the weary wheel aside,
The fairest of the four, I ween.

They're glancing through the glimmer of the quiet eve,
Away in milky wavings of neck and ankle bare;
The heavy-sliding stream in its sleepy song they leave,
And the crags in the ghostly air:

And linking hand in hand, and singing as they go,
The maids along the hill-side have ta'en their fearless way,
Till they come to where the rowan trees in lonely beauty grow
Beside the Fairy Hawthorn grey.

The Hawthorn stands between the ashes tall and slim,
Like matron with her twin grand-daughters at her knee;
The rowan berries cluster o'er her low head grey and dim
In ruddy kisses sweet to see.

The merry maidens four have ranged them in a row,
Between each lovely couple a stately rowan stem,
And away in mazes wavy, like skimming birds they go,
Oh, never caroll'd bird like them!

But solemn is the silence of the silvery haze
That drinks away their voices in echoless repose,
And dreamily the evening has still'd the haunted braes,
And dreamier the gloaming grows.

And sinking one by one, like lark-notes from the sky

76

When the falcon's shadow saileth across the open shaw,
Are hush'd the maiden's voices, as cowering down they he
In the flutter of their sudden awe.

For, from the air above, the grassy ground beneath,
And from the mountain-ashes and the old Whitethorn between,
A Power of faint enchantment doth through their beings
breathe,
And they sink down together on the green.

They sink together silent, and stealing side by side,
They fling their lovely arms o'er their drooping necks so fair,
Then vainly strive again their naked arms to hide,
For their shrinking necks again are bare.

Thus clasp'd and prostrate all, with their heads together bow'd,
Soft o'er their bosom's beating--the only human sound--
They hear the silky footsteps of the silent fairy crowd,
Like a river in the air, gliding round.

No scream can any raise, no prayer can any say,
But wild, wild, the terror of the speechless three--
For they feel fair Anna Grace drawn silently away,
By whom they dare not look to see.

They feel their tresses twine with her parting locks of gold
And the curls elastic falling as her head withdraws;
They feel her sliding arms from their tranced arms unfold,
But they may not look to see the cause:

For heavy on their senses the faint enchantment lies
Through all that night of anguish and perilous amaze;
And neither fear nor wonder can ope their quivering eyes,
Or their limbs from the cold ground raise,

Till out of night the earth has roll'd her dewy side,
With every haunted mountain and streamy vale below;
When, as the mist dissolves in the yellow morning tide,

The maidens' trance dissolveth go.

Then fly the ghastly three as swiftly as they may,
And tell their tale of sorrow to anxious friends in vain--
They pined away and died within the year and day,
And ne'er was Anna Grace seen again.

By Sir Samuel Ferguson

Belfast Fairy Trees & Wells

Belfast had its fair share of fairy thorns before the city spread out. One such tree existed in Divis Street and in a fairy ring near the Whitewell. Fairy Wells were located in the Bog Meadows near Balmoral. It was said that their water was always ice-cold even on a hot summer's day. 'Monday's Well' was a famous fairy well in Sandy Row from which, through wooden pipes, the fountain in Fountain Street was supplied with water. Another well was near the Crumlin Road Court House. Once an old public house was located nearby and it was aptly named 'The Fairy Well Tavern'.

Fairy House at Maghera, Newcastle

It is said that if one damages the home of a fairy then bad luck will also befall the perpetrator. Many years ago, a Maghera woman told the tale of how her great grandmother received a visit from a tiny old woman who warned her not to build a turf stack in a certain spot. She explained that if the stack was erected the chimneys of her little house would be damaged. However, her warning was ignored and the farmers built the turf stack in the original place. Not long afterwards four of the farmers cows died suspiciously.

Fairy Fort, Glasdrumman

It is also bad luck to destroy or damage fairy forts as it was believed that the fairies lived in the soutterains underneath the forts or raths as they are also known. One such fort near Glasdrumman was demolished by the owner of the land on which it was located with the help of several other men. The story goes that the man who struck the first blow was injured and he died very shortly afterwards. A local woman who lived close by the fort alleged that on the evening after it was destroyed she heard loud cries and wails coming from the direction of the former fort. She believed that this was the fairies weeping as they departed from their home.

Baby Snatchers, Belfast

This story is about a young girl who lived near North Queen Street. She was asked to help her aunt who had just had a baby boy. The new baby was initially very healthy and happy but after a few days it became very sickly and cross and cried incessantly. The girl had noticed a change in the baby and became convinced that the baby had in fact been taken away by the fairies and replaced by a 'girnin wasp'.

She went to take advice from a wise old woman who lived nearby. The old woman called to see the baby and gave the girl important instructions. She was told to get three bracken leaves and place them near the baby's cradle, one on each side and the remaining one at the foot. Then she had to take a bible and place it at the head of the cradle. Just before midnight, she had to place one of her hands on the bible and gently hold the baby's throat and command the real child to be replaced and the fairy to depart. As the old woman was describing these instructions, the existing 'baby' changed colour and began to scream.

When night came, the girl prepared the setting and just when the clock started to chime at midnight, her uncle arrived at the house and began knocking the door. The girl had to get up and let him in. While she was doing this, the 'change' took place and the horrible fairy fled away on the bracken leaves. The girl ran to the cradle and was greatly relieved to find that the healthy baby boy had returned. She was overjoyed. She claimed that later on she heard the fairies laughing at the back of the fairy mound in Duncairn.

Fairy Woman in Laurencetown

A housekeeper had just finished her daily tasks in one of the large houses in the area and decided to go out and meet her friends nearby. She locked up the empty house with her key and walked down the driveway. On her early return she was very shocked to see a tiny old woman sitting warming herself by the kitchen fire. The woman was almost grey in colour and frightened the life out of the housekeeper. She asked the woman, *"Who are you and how did you get in?"* The old lady made no reply and just sat there looking at the fire. Very scared, the housekeeper ran out and therefore did not see where the old lady went to or how she left the house. The housekeeper decided that she could no longer return to that house and she handed in her notice with immediate effect. She is adamant that she actually saw a fairy woman.

Fairy Story in Maghera, Newcastle

One day a farmer and his young son went out to work in the fields. The boy was around four or five years old. He was not able to help his father much so he lay down in the grass while his father worked. After some time, the father heard a loud noise and as he looked back towards his son, he saw several little men about two feet high, dancing around him.

The father shouted at the little men and as he ran towards them he demanded they go away and leave his son alone. They stopped their dancing and ran towards a local fort and then they suddenly disappeared. His young son appeared to be alright but the family soon discovered that he was deaf. The unfortunate boy's hearing did return after ten years or so but he died at the very young age of seventeen years. The family believed that the fairies had put a spell on the boy that day in the field some years earlier.

Fairy Story in Maghera, Newcastle

Fairies of Piping Rock, Ballyhornan

Piping Rock lies close to the sea near Crunglass, Ballyhornan on the County Down coast. As its name implies, this is an area where music is played and in this particular case the music was practised by the 'little folk' or the fairies.

To find the rock the passerby had to leave the road and walk down a long winding path edged by high flower covered hedges. This in turn led to a grassy bank before the grey gorse covered rock appeared blocking the path. Many years ago, it is said that the old people of the area would listen to the fairy music during long summer evenings.

In the late 1920s, a local lad was out walking his dog in Leggykinney close to the Piping Rock. As he approached and looked down a little valley, he was surprised to see a little man about two and half feet tall. He was wearing a red suit, a pixie hat and black buckled shoes. The boy's dog ran down to the little man but he stood still and never made a sound. The boy called his dog back but it would not come to him. Scared by the sight of the little man, the boy decided to run home on his own. He was excited to tell his family about the strange little man but was dismayed when no-one would believe him except his uncle who had seen one or two fairies over the years.

Another story from the same area involves a farmer who was about to tether his cow in a certain spot in Crunglass when suddenly a voice was heard instructing him not to do so. The farmer ignored the warning and the next morning when he went to check on his cow, he found it lying dead!

Such fairy haunts are now overgrown as the passing years have taken their toll and are almost forgotten about.

Fairies Seen in Ballydrummond, Castlewellan

Many years ago, a local girl claimed to have seen a fairy at her uncle's house one Sunday morning. She explained that she saw a tiny red woman coming down the lane towards her uncle's house. She hid and watched as the 'wee woman', who was about three feet high, entered the cottage by the front door. Her uncle was an invalid and was in the house on his own that particular day. The girl continued hiding until the fairy woman left. Later on that day, her uncle asked her if she had seen anything strange. The girl was too frightened and lied saying that she had not seen a thing. Her uncle then said that his visitor was a fairy woman and that he had given her a penny.

In the same area, a neighbour also saw some fairies. They were singing and dancing. *"See-saw, bow-bell. Hook an' eye, bow-bell"* were the words they sang.

Another neighbour told this story. An old lady lived with her daughter-in-law in a small country cottage. Whenever the old lady went away to visit and stay with her own daughter who had married and was living elsewhere, fairies would come into the house and remove all her bed-clothes from her bed. This prevented the daughter-in-law, who the fairies did not like, from sleeping in that comfortable bed. Each time, just before the woman returned home, the bedclothes would reappear on the bed.

Fairies in Annalong

An old lady from Annalong claimed that she and her sister often saw fairies when they were young girls. She described them as small in stature about the size of a child of seven or eight years of age.

Another Annalong girl once found a tiny slate coloured glove on the window sill of her home. It was so small it did not fit over her thumb but it was embroidered in intricate detail. The girl took the glove to a wise old man who lived close by. He advised her that it was a fairy glove and that it should go back to the exact place where it was found. The girl followed his instructions and very soon after, the glove disappeared.

To this day, the woman believes that the fairy who had mislaid the glove came back and reclaimed it.

The Kilkeel Pooka Story

This story comes from Aughnahoory just outside Kilkeel. A local man 'Robbey the Rake' used to cross the Pookey Bridge every night to play cards with his friend Frank in Aughnahoory. A 'Pooka' or 'Fairy Horse' was well known for hiding under the bridge at night. Many of his friends tried to stop Robbey from crossing the bridge but he would not listen to their warnings. He enjoyed the 'craic' and jokes at Frank's house too much to take another route.

One particular night after midnight, Robbey was returning home and was halfway across the bridge when he met a well-dressed gentleman although his lower limbs could not be seen. He asked Robbey for a game of cards but he refused as he just wanted to get home. The other man then just disappeared and Robbey suddenly found himself on the back of a 'Pooka'. The wild animal shrieked and started to gallop towards a nearby gorge.

Poor Robbey fought hard to stay on its back and tightly held on to the horse's mane. The horse galloped through briars, bogs, flax dams and then headed to Slieve Binnian. Onward they went up and down all the peaks of the Mourne Mountains and when it reached Lough Shannagh, it jumped out of the black water. They rode to Knockcree and then Greencastle. By this time Robbey was soaked through with sweat and covered in mud. When they reached Cranfield, all this was washed way as they galloped in the sea. Onwards they continued to Dunavil Fort and then back to Kilkeel to the Manse Strand.

"Would you like to be dropped here?" Asked the beast. *"No"* replied Robbey as they were just outside the local priest's house and he was scared of what he would say about his gambling habit.

The beast eventually took him back to the Pookey Bridge and left him off there. Robbey managed to recover somewhat and went home a changed man. From that night on he never played cards again and stayed in his own house beside the fire. His wife Bella never learned the reason why!

The Fairy Mid-Wife, Hilltown

There was once a midwife who lived between Hilltown and Rathfriland. She was renowned for being very good at her job and would often be called out at all hours to help with the delivery of babies in the area.

One night she answered the door to a strange little man who was dressed all in black. He pleaded with her to come with him to help his wife who was in labour. He pointed to his large grey horse and the two saddles on its back. The mid-wife was not too sure about accompanying the little man but he became very distressed and begged her even more to attend his wife. Finally she agreed and she was helped onto the big horse.

They travelled at a very fast pace on this magnificent animal and galloped over mountains, valleys and lakes until at long last they came to a magnificent castle. The drawbridge was lowered and they entered. Immediately the mid-wife was taken upstairs to the man's wife who was already in labour. Eventually a healthy baby boy was delivered and everyone was well. Afterwards, the mid-wife was taken downstairs to a huge dining hall where a crowd had gathered to feast the birth. After sitting down, she looked all around and was surprised to recognise one of the guests. She was a young neighbour who had died several years earlier. Upon seeing the mid-wife, the young former seamstress came over to her very quietly and whispered in her ear not to eat or drink anything as she would be put under a spell and would never be allowed to leave the castle.

The mid-wife did as she was told and refused all food and drink. After some time, she was summoned to be taken home and the strange pair once again sat on the mighty horse as they galloped the same route home again. Dismounting, the little man asked her never to repeat this story to anyone, not even her husband. Her adventure had to be kept a secret. When she entered her house, she put her hands in her pockets and found that they were full of gold coins. Immediately, she hid them in a secret box away from her family.

As time went on, her husband kept asking her where she had been and if she had been rewarded for her services and although she replied that nothing had happened, he started to mock her and called her a liar. She was so infuriated at her husband that in a fit of anger and frustration, she told him the whole story and then went to show him the wooden box full of gold coins.

However when she opened the box, it was empty! As she had broken her promise by telling her story, the fairies had taken back their gold.

Fairies at Tollymore

An elderly lady was convinced that fairies existed and related this story about fairies near Tollymore Park, Newcastle. Some years earlier, she lived nearby on a farm. One day she went outside to tend her goat and its kid. Suddenly she heard shouting and screaming coming from the direction of the hills. She went closer to the noise and could not believe her eyes as she observed a group of tiny people dancing. They had red spiky hair and were scantily dressed.

Another neighbour friend also spoke of the fairies in the

same area. One day she was sitting alone in her cottage when a tiny old woman entered and borrowed a bowl of meal from her meal barrel. The neighbour noticed that immediately the missing meal was replaced. Each day whatever meal she used was replenished the next morning.

She believed that the fairy woman had rewarded her by continually filling up the barrel. She kept this a secret from her family.

One day her husband asked if she needed any more meal as he was going to the market. He was surprised when she said she had plenty left. He queried this as he knew that the meal barrel should have been almost empty by this stage. He kept asking her to explain. Eventually she told him the story of the fairy visitor but when she went to show him the full barrel, she discovered that it was in fact empty! She realised that she should have kept the fairy story a secret.

Lisnacroppan Cave

Lisnacroppan lies in the Parish of Annaclone a few miles from Rathfriland. This particular story was handed down through the Clan Magennis who once ruled most of County Down. It starts with a young boy and girl who were seeing each other and were out one summer's day for a walk. The girl ran into a nearby cave to hide from her boyfriend who was called Hugh Magennis.

Unluckily for the girl, an old witch lived in the cave and she became very jealous of the young girl and her beautiful looks. The witch placed a spell on the girl so that if she ever left the cave, she would suddenly turn into an ugly old hag and no man would ever want her. The young girl was therefore forced to remain in the cave for the rest of her days and she roamed from one end of the cave at Lisnacroppan to the other end which was located at Ballynanny, another townland in Annaclone.

The cave was called 'the witch's curse' and some people say that one can still hear the young girl's cries as her spirit roams the cave looking to escape especially in the summer months. There are also stories of sheep going missing in these caves and never being seen again. Who abducts the sheep? One wonders.

Lisnacroppan Cave

Fairy Gold

Many years ago in an isolated part of County Down there lived a poor farmer and his wife. The man had a very strange dream three nights in a row and he was very puzzled by it. In his dream he found a sack of fairy gold under the roots of a lone bush near to his cottage.

After the third night of having the same dream, he decided to do something about it and look for the sack. That evening, when no-one was about, he stepped outside with his spade and started to dig up the soil near the single bush. Soon his spade struck against something hard and he dug even harder. He had found a sack! Lifting it from the soil, he noticed that it was indeed very heavy! Was it full of gold coins? He managed to drag the sack into his byre out of view. His wife was with him and they both were getting very excited with their find and the thought of all the wealth the sack would bring to their lives.

"Did you spit on the sack?" She inquired. *"I did not!"* replied the farmer. His wife then became quite anxious and she explained that the fairy gold was enchanted and the only way to keep it was to spit on it. But the farmer would not listen to her warning and ignoring her concerns he started to open the sack. Even the cows in the byre started to become distressed and try to break free from their places.

The farmer and his wife then noticed that the bag had started to move and she began to scream and the cows started to stamp and roar. Her husband continued to ignore them and he opened the sack fully.

Inside the sack was a giant eel with eyes the colour of flames. It wriggled out of the sack and then reared up into the air and then disappeared through the thatched roof. The poor couple were left speechless! So much for their fairy gold!

Crooked Jack

Many years ago a poor basket maker lived in County Down. He was known as 'Crooked Jack' although no-one knows if 'Jack' was his right name. He was so named as he had a large hump on his back which caused his head to press down and force his chin onto his chest. The Gaelic for 'hunchback' is 'cruiteachán' and this may have been translated as 'Crooked Jack'.

Crooked Jack was a very kind and sociable man and everyone used to like meeting him as he travelled throughout the county selling his wares. One particular hot summer's day as he walked the roads, he became very tired as he had difficulty walking and decided to rest near an ancient mound.

As he rested, he soon began to hear sweet music coming from within the mound. He became very happy and began to hum to the tunes. Suddenly he found himself being picked up and within seconds found he was inside the mound. He was surrounded by a large group of dancing fairies. He was amazed at this sight and smiled and laughed at their antics. When the music stopped, the fairies huddled together and talked among themselves for a while.

One of the fairies approached Crooked Jack and said *"Crooked Jack, the hump that you bore, you will have no more. See it fall to the floor"*

Jack did feel a lot lighter and found himself straighten. He began to lift his head and for the first time in his life, he was able to stand tall. His hump was gone!

He felt very dizzy and fell to the ground and into a deep sleep. The next morning he awoke with the sun and remembering what had happened, he looked for his hump but it was definitely gone. What is more the fairies had dressed him in a new suit and shoes. He could not believe his luck and was so grateful. He went on his journey with a spring in his step.

People hardly recognised the new Jack and wondered how he had managed to lose his hump. Word spread around the area quickly about his amazing good fortune.

One day a lady approached Jack and asked him all the details of his story. She informed Jack that her friend's son also had a hump and that it would be a good idea for him to try to reach the fairies as well so that his hump would also disappear.

The story was then passed on to her friend's son who was called Mick Rooney. Very soon after, Mick set off to the fairy mound and sat down beside it to listen out for the fairy music. True to Jack's story, he started to hear the sweet music coming from within the mound. Rather than enjoying the music, Mick started immediately to join in as he was a very impatient man. He was out of tune and he roared and shouted very loudly. He had thought that if he shouted really loudly, the fairies might grant him two new suits of clothes rather than just the one given to Crooked Jack.

His shouts made it difficult to even hear the fairy music, but like Crooked Jack, he found himself soon inside the mound. However, the fairies were very angry with him and asked *"Why are you spoiling our song?"* one fairy continued *"Mick, you are so bad that we will make you sick, two humps now for you, Mick!"* With that, a group of fairies took Crooked Jack's hump and stuck it on his back!

The next day, his mother and her friend found Mick with the two humps. They both tried to pull off the new hump but without success. They all left for home and cursed the fairies and anyone who dared to go and listen to fairy music. Poor Mick had two humps for the rest of his life.

Chapter 4

Haunted Places

The Ballyroney Lake Ghost

"When I'm asked 'Are you afraid of the dark?', my answer is 'No, I'm afraid of what is in the dark."

Barry Fitzgerald

The Phantom Sower, Hilltown

This story was experienced by a group of young people returning from a dance in the then recently opened INF Hall in Hilltown. It was in the 1950s when cars were few and walking was not uncommon, even at night.

The area concerned was called 'The Stand Tops' and it lay high up behind the 'Mourneview bar' situated on the Kilkeel road out of Hilltown. Many hundreds of years earlier the land was owned by the landed gentry. Legend has it that two lads set out to sow a field of corn. They had a serious row which sadly ended in one of them killing the other. Panicking, the killer buried his victim in the hope that he would not be found out. However, he was soon caught and then hanged for his crime.

The ghost of his victim 'the phantom sower' had apparently been seen from time to time on moonlight nights still walking with the white bag apron spreading the seed corn.

On this particular bright moonlight night, the dancers made their way home. One member of their party had decided to leave earlier and dress up as the phantom sower to scare his friends. He was wearing a white bag apron and was actually in a field on the Stang Tops as his friends passed by.

All of a sudden his friends started screaming in terror and pointed at him to look behind. Turning round and to his horror there was the real phantom sower approaching towards him.

Yelling with fear he threw off the apron and at a speed that would do an Olympic athlete proud, he reached his friends on the road. Needless to say that put an end to him ever again trying to emulate the ghost of the phantom sower!

The Ballyroney Lake Ghost

Many years ago a brother and sister lived together in a farm at Ballyroney. They were very attached to one another and neither wanted anything more from life than the happy companionship and goodwill which they shared.

However a young man came into the girl's life and he fell in love with her. She of course was thrilled and returned this love. They planned to get married and perhaps then move to a different locality. Her brother forbade her to marry her fiancé and in fact he did not allow her to see him again. The girl was broken hearted and as the days, months and years rolled on, she became thin and listless. By this time the unfortunate young fiancé had emigrated. At last the girl could go on no longer and one night she crept out and drowned herself in Ballyroney Lake.

Her brother was to pay in more ways than one for his callous action. His sister's ghost haunted him every night till at length he went to the Scotch Harvest and hoped that going to a different country would lay the ghost. But while he was on the ship, his sister haunted him throughout the harvest.

When he sailed back to Ireland, his sister's ghost sailed with him. He knew now that it was quite hopeless to think of peace again. He was an absolute bundle of nerves and so eventually one night he too went down to the Lake in Ballyroney and drowned himself.

Haunted Field At Knockavally, Killough

There is a haunted field just outside Killough in an area called Knockavally. There is a mound in the middle of the field with a large stone which has an old Irish Cross engraved into it. Local people claim that the cross marks the site of an ancient graveyard and that the field is haunted by spirits of the long dead. It is a place where the faint hearted should not go on their own. Tradition states that if one rotates the cross face downwards, the next day, the cross will have returned to its original position.

Many years ago when the horse and cart was the main mode of transport in the area, the horses used to be frightened, pawing at the ground and refusing to pass the field and many had to be blind folded. Many believed that animals especially horses, were sensitive to the world of ghosts and spirits.

One story relates to a local man who was out shooting ducks in a nearby bog. He waited for the ducks to fly into the field and when they appeared he managed to shoot two of them and watched as they fell from the sky into the field. When he went to look for them there was no sign of the ducks and even more mysterious, he seemed to be lost in the field as he could not find his way out. A fog descended on the field as he searched in vain for the gate by which he entered the field. Eventually he heard some men laughing and joking as they passed by. He cried out for help but no one heard him! He was lost in the haunted field!

He reloaded his shotgun and fired twice in the air hoping that someone would respond to the gunfire. Suddenly the mist and fog lifted and he could clearly see lamps in the windows of nearby cottages close by. A voice called out, *"What's wrong?"* The man replied that he could not get out of the field. The others started laughing and answered back, *"You can get out of the field over there, the gate in front of you"*. Suddenly everything was clear and he could see the entrance gate quite clearly. He quickly climbed over the gate and told the others about his ordeal. Two of the others started to tell him that this field was indeed 'Holy Ground' and that he should not be in the field on his own and especially with a shotgun.

The stone with the engraved cross is now displayed in Down County Museum for safe keeping.

The Mysterious Moving Barrel of Dechomet

One sunny day in the summer of 1988, a local man was busy in his farm. He was stacking hay from his tractor and trailer into the loft of his hayshed.

He decided to take a rest from this arduous work and sat down on the top of some hay bales on the tractor. It was such a beautiful day, without as much as a breeze and he calmly looked around the farmyard and then over the top of the cab of the tractor. He noticed a 40 gallon empty barrel standing upright in the bottom part of the yard. The yard sloped at a 15-20 degrees angle. He could not believe his eyes when the barrel decided to fall over on its side and move up the slope of the yard. Thinking someone was pushing the barrel he jumped up in amazement for a better view but there was no one else in the yard and there was no wind. The next thing he observed was the barrel reaching the top of the yard and positioning itself tight against the barn wall. After a second or two, it started to roll back down the yard but only for two or three feet. It suddenly stopped and then spun round 180 degrees so it could no longer roll down the yard.

To this day the farmer cannot explain this phenomenon. It seemed as if there was an invisible presence pushing the barrel as there was certainly no wind or breeze in the air.

The Mysterious Moving Barrel of Dechomet

The Slieve Donard Hawker

This story appeared in the Mourne Observer some years ago and was provided by a Newcastle reader who had heard it from his great uncle. The story was about an old hunter from the Mournes named Drew Hall. He was nick-named the Hawker as he always had a hooded hawk on his arm even when he was drinking in a local tavern.

One particular night, a row started in the tavern between an old immigrant and the captain of the local bowls team. The immigrant had just lost his job and had also been dropped from the bowling team. The immigrant started to fight with the other man but was being beaten in the brawl. The Hawker decided to let his hawk loose and it attacked the bowls captain and ended up killing him in front of everyone in the tavern.

The Hawker and the badly injured immigrant managed to make their escape into the stormy night. They were wanted men and were searched for everywhere. Even soldiers were deployed for this purpose in the Mourne Mountains but they were never found.

It is believed that the Hawker took the immigrant to the top of Slieve Donard where they 'flew into the gale' and ended up in Lisbon, Portugal where the immigrant had come from originally. There they settled and never returned to Ireland again. But it is said that during every winter's gale, around Christmas time, the Hawker can often be seen standing at the top of Slieve Donard with the immigrant in his arms and his hawk on his shoulder.

Haunted Road in Laurencetown

As one passes Laurencetown on the way to Seapatrick, do not be surprised if you see some strange figures wandering along that road late at night.

One night during the 1960s around one in the morning a woman called Evans was coming home to Banbridge after attending a dance in Tullylish Hall. As she drove past an old mill, she suddenly found herself driving behind a funeral. A tall man with a horse drawn hearse and two black horses had come onto the road in front of her. She had to slow down to a walking pace as she continued to follow the funeral cortege. She could hardly believe that this was happening at such a late hour. After about one hundred yards the cortege turned off the road to the right and disappeared.

When her car reached this spot, she observed that it would have been impossible to follow the funeral as there was a high fence and a thick hedge. There was no opening. Later on the woman told her story to a number of people and was surprised to hear that the same thing had happened to other drivers along this stretch of the road. No-one could explain this mysterious sighting.

This was not the only ghostly event to happen in this area. Many other people have witnessed a hooded figure crossing the road in front of them at the junction of the Broken Bridge and the Lurgan Road. The figure resembles a lightly built teenager or a child. The figure does not look right or left as it swiftly crosses the junction. It then is seen disappearing through a wall on the side of the road. Years earlier, a young person was knocked down and killed crossing the road at this particular spot. Could this be its ghost coming back to haunt the area?

Haunted Road in Laurencetown

Blue Lady of Tollymore

Another 'Blue Lady Ghost' is said to haunt the Forest Park at Tollymore. Apparently the lady used to live in the old seat of the Roden family in Tollymore House. Her former home was demolished after the war. She wanders restlessly now looking for her old home and she has been seen gliding up and down the tree lined avenue.

A Dream

I Heard the dogs howl in the moonlight night;

I went to the window to see the sight;

All the Dead that ever I knew

Going one by one and two by two.

On they pass'd, and on they pass'd;

Townsfellows all, from first to last;

Born in the moonlight of the lane,

Quench'd in the heavy shadow again.

Schoolmates, marching as when we play'd

At soldiers once-but no more staid;

Those were the strangest sight to me

Who were drown'd, I knew, in the awful sea.

Straight and handsome fold; bent and weak, too;

Some that I loved, and gasp'd to speak to;

Some but a day in their churchyard bed;

Some that I had not known were dead.

A long, long crowd- where each seem'd lonely,

Yet of them all there was one, one only,

Raised a head or look'd my way.

She linger'd a moment,-she might not stay.

How long since I saw that fair pale face!

Ah! Mother dear! Might I only place

My head on thy breast, a moment to rest,

While thy hand on my tearful cheek were prest!

On, on, a moving bridge they made

Across the moon-stream, from shade to shade,

Young and old, women and men;

Many long-forgot, but remember'd then.

And first there came a bitter laughter;

A sound of tears the moment after;

And then a music so lofty and gay,

That every morning, day by day,

I strive to recall it if I may.

By William Allingham

The Phantom Football Match

Years ago two friends were riding their horses past an old church. One of the horses suddenly stopped at the churchyard gates and would not move any further. It seemed to be frozen to the spot. Deciding that there was something going on in the graveyard, the friends dismounted and went in through the gates.

They could not believe their eyes when they saw a football match taking place with a crowd of spectators gathered to cheer them on. But the players and the crowd were all the spirits of the deceased whose last resting place was the graveyard. Wanting to get home, one of the men shouted out that he had to get his horse released. He was approached by one of the footballers and was told that his horse could not move until the game was over. He added that his team was a man short as they had been waiting for someone from the next parish to die but he was taking his time.

One of the men stated that his granny was from there and this then qualified him to play for the team. He offered to volunteer and get the game over as soon as possible so that he could get home. It did not bother him that he was the only mortal footballer among so many spirits of the dead.

The match then officially began and it was a very close game with only one point between the two scores. Just before the final whistle, the mortal picked up the ball and ran down the graveyard and scored the winning goal. His team were very happy and there were loud cheers from the crowd and he was hailed as a hero by all.

Now all he wanted was to leave but his team captain insisted on making a speech.

"My boy, our great regret is that there are no medals for this game we have just played". He continued, *"We are unanimous*

*about one thing. We do not want to lose our star player and we
have decided that in view of the splendid game you have just
played tonight, that you are to be here as a permanent player
from next Sunday!".*

The Phantom Football Match

The Ghost of the Diamond

As one travels along the main Rathfriland Road from
Banbridge one comes to a junction known as 'The Diamond'.
On the right-hand side of the road there stands the ruins of
an old house. This house is alleged to be haunted and many
a passer-by has claimed to have heard strange noises from
inside. The noise is supposed to emanate from the ghost of a
child that used to live there and resembles someone rattling a
tin and a spoon.

Apparently many years ago the family that resided in the
house had a disabled child. In years gone by, disability was

frowned upon and seen as a punishment from God. The family were ashamed of their child to the extent that they kept it out of sight and locked up. The hidden child never saw the light of day and ended up dying in one of the rooms. Its only plaything was a spoon and a tin which the child used to bang together. Its ghost now haunts the house and makes this same noise.

Weeping Ghost of Bogey Hill, Newcastle

Another haunted part of Newcastle is Bogey Hill. The haunting commenced after the tragic local fishing disaster of 1843 when so many Newcastle and Annalong men lost their lives at sea. The ghost is a sorrowful woman dressed in black who stands on Bogey Hill looking into the sea. She has been seen sobbing and waiting for the return of her long, lost husband. Others have seen a male ghost also dressed in black in the same area. Could this be the husband of the sobbing female ghost?

Apparition in Derryleckagh

Many years ago, a local man was walking the last few miles to his home in Derryleckagh. It was a very stormy night and he passed the deserted ruins of an old cottage which was supposedly haunted. It was said that the occupant had murdered his wife and daughter before hanging himself. The two women were buried in a local church graveyard while the man was taken to a nearby marsh.

All of a sudden he was halted and a deathly coldness came over his entire body. Out of the old cottage appeared a ghostly figure and it appeared to be floating towards him. It was translucent and covered in a long white flowing garment. The old man started to pray as he backed away from the spectre but it kept advancing towards him. He was somehow forced up a lane leading to another cottage which was occupied by two young girls whose mother had recently passed away. He kept thinking to himself that he could not disturb these girls as they would be sleeping and he did not want to frighten them.

Facing the spectre he shouted, *"What do you want?"* He could not believe his eyes when the spectre appeared to dissolve and then turn into a large white rabbit. But it continued to try to force him towards the girls' cottage. Deciding it best not to look at the rabbit, he covered his eyes and zigzagged back down the lane to the road and avoided looking at the rabbit.

Using this method he managed to get past both cottages and he kept going and did not dare to look back. Eventually he got home to his own house and exhausted he fell asleep. The next morning as he had his breakfast, his front door opened and a distressed neighbour entered. He informed the man that during the night, an old beech tree had blown down on top of the girls' cottage as they slept. Both girls were killed.

The old man became very distressed to hear this bad news. He then realised that the spectre was simply trying to get him up the lane to the girls' cottage and waken them. Their lives may have been saved from the falling tree. The reason why the apparition turned into a rabbit was so that the old man would be less frightened.

However the old man did not realise that at the time and because he was so stubborn, the poor girls' fate was sealed.

Mystery Man in Slievenaman, Mournes

Some years ago five hill walkers were exploring the hills around Spelga Dam. As they clambered over Slievenaman, one of the walkers fell and hurt himself. The rest of the group managed to carry him to a nearby cottage where he could shelter while they went for help. A fire was lit in the old hearth and he was made as comfortable as possible. While the hill walker remained in the cottage and waited for help, he had a visitor. It was an elderly man who kept him company and chatted to him for several hours. The hill walker then fell asleep.

Eventually the others came back with help. They asked if he had been lonely waiting for them and he told them about the old man who had now vanished. They asked if he knew who this mystery companion was and he described him. One of the party of helpers was a local man and he became very surprised at hearing the description. It was another local Slievenaman resident who had died a couple of years earlier. Everyone, especially the injured hill walker was very surprised to hear this.

The Newry Graveyard Baby

This story originates from a football match being played by a group of friends near a graveyard in Newry in the 1930s. The ball was accidently kicked over the wall into the graveyard. Most of the boys decided that they would not enter the graveyard to retrieve the ball and so it was up to its owner to venture inside. He certainly did not want to leave his ball behind. He climbed over the wall and started to look for his property. Eventually he located the ball near one of the oldest headstones. He noticed a strange design imprinted on the stone and to his surprise, he came across a small baby beside it. Thinking that the baby was dead, he left it there.

As the days went by, the boy started to think about the baby and also worry about its wellbeing. His mind started to play tricks and the image of the baby would appear in his dreams and also at night while he was in bed. This type of haunting continued over the years and the boy became very unwell as a consequence. People say that he never really got over his encounter and he died young.

It was decided to bury him beside the headstone where the baby was first seen. One of the local gravediggers admitted that he would never approach these graves as one would hear the sound of a baby's cry.

Shortcut Through Castlewellan Graveyard

One clear night, a local man was hurrying home and decided to take a short cut through the graveyard in Castlewellan. He overheard a chipping noise as he weaved his way through the headstones. He listened carefully and followed the noise until he saw the figure of a man leaning over one particular headstone as he chipped away. He asked this man what he was doing so late at night in the graveyard. The man replied, *"They have spelt my name wrong"*

The local man ran as fast as he could out of the graveyard frightened out of his wits!

Ghost of Baillies Bridge, Bryansford

In Bryansford during the 1930s a middle aged woman was cycling home one day after visiting her friend. As she approached Baillies Bridge, she could go no further, her bicycle had just come to a halt and would not budge. She could not get across the bridge. The woman returned to her friend's house and told her what had happened. They then decided to contact the local priest. After he heard the story, they all approached the bridge once more and the priest began to say some prayers. He then left a bottle on the bridge declaring that the spirit of the bridge was now trapped inside it. He left instructions that the bottle was to be built into the wall of the bridge and it remains there to this day.

Since then there have been no more reports of people being prevented from crossing over the bridge.

Narrow Water Castle near Warrenpoint

The Ghosts of Narrow Water Castle

Narrow Water Castle is reputed to be haunted by a squire who was cursed by a local priest. Many years ago, the priest was given a brutal whipping by the squire and afterwards the priest cursed him to choke to death as a punishment. It is claimed that the ghost of the squire can be heard crying out with a dreadful gurgling sound similar to that of a person who is indeed choking.

Another story relates to the ghosts of soldiers being seen on the road between Newry and Warrenpoint near Narrow Water Castle. In August 1979, eighteen soldiers were killed during a two-stage bomb planted by the IRA. The attack was carried out as a convoy of two army trucks made its way from an army base in Newry. Its route took it past the castle. An 800 Lb. bomb was hidden in a trailer at the side of the road concealed among bales of straw. It detonated as the rear convoy passed by. It is believed that six soldiers died in the first explosion. The remainder were killed by a second explosion as they took up a defence position behind nearby gates and a wall.

Since then many motorists passing through that area have claimed to have seen soldiers standing at the side of the road. Some have even pulled into the hard shoulder thinking that it was an actual checkpoint. When they reach the side of the road there is no-one there! On another occasion a man pulled in and got out of his car to go to the toilet and when he looked around there was a soldier beside him. Needless to say he did not take the time to zip his trousers before getting back into his car!

Another Ghost in Greencastle

After de Burgh, the castle at Greencastle was passed to the Magennis's, then to Nicholas Bagnal and eventually to the Needham family. It is now in ruins but many ghost stories are attached to this old castle. Centuries ago, a ship from a strange land was seen to dock at Greencastle Pier. A very small man came ashore alone and made his way to the castle. However, he was never seen leaving or in fact never seen again so no-one knows of his fate.

After midnight following his arrival, everything in the castle went berserk. All the animals started roaring, pots and pans rattled and old clock fell from a wall to the ground. This commotion continued every night until the local clergy decided to carry out an exorcism. Whatever or whoever was causing the noise was ordered to be banished from the area for at least 520 years. The spirit was not happy about this but the clergy stuck to their original demand.

No-one knows what will happen when the 520 years expires and some say that this event will happen very soon.

Ghost Lights Up Sky in Ballysheil, Annaclone

This is a country area where neighbours would regularly help each other especially at busy times of the year, for example, potato gathering or at harvest time. One local lad then aged about sixteen tells this story about when he used to help his farmer neighbour by feeding his cattle or sheep or whatever else was needed. One particular warm summer's day, the boy and the farmer worked late to bring in his hay. It was nearly eleven at night when the farmer thanked his helper and suggested that the boy should make his way home as it was getting too dark to ride his bike and see the road.

He did not live far up the road and so he began to cycle home. The boy had travelled this road many times and was quite familiar with all the bends and hills. However, he had also heard stories about the road being haunted so he peddled as fast as he could and soon saw the lights of his own home in the distance.

As he travelled downhill the bicycle began to pick up speed and he took his feet off the pedals. Suddenly a bright light lit up the road in front of him as if it was a beam of light from the sky. He could not understand where the light had come from but as he got closer, he could see what seemed to be a dark shadow or figure in the middle of the light. The figure resembled that of a very tall man wearing what appeared to be a bowler hat.

The young man was terrified but because he was going at such a speed he could not stop and not having any brakes on the bike did not help. He travelled straight through the figure.

The only thing the boy felt was a cold sensation enveloping his body as he passed through the figure. When he managed to stop and turn around, the light had gone and the road was once again in darkness. There was so sign of the figure.

The boy is now in his forties and still remembers this event very well as it was one of the strangest things that ever happened to him. He still lives on this very road and whenever he is driving past that particular point in the road, he often thinks about that summer's night. He remains convinced that the figure was indeed a ghost but has no idea of whose ghost it was.

Ghost Lights Up Sky in Ballysheil, Annaclone

Tyrella Beach Ghost

During World War Two, a Belfast family were evacuated to County Down where they had managed to find an old cottage along the beach in Tyrella. It was an isolated cottage with no electricity or running water but the children loved staying there and when the parents returned to Belfast the older teenagers remained in the cottage for the rest of the summer. One of the boys became aware of something or someone watching him from the corner of his bedroom. He was not particularly frightened by this apparition but was very curious about it. He later discovered that the figure was that of a young girl who had drowned on a Sunday School excursion to the beach several years previously. The body had been left in the same cottage overnight before being removed.

At night, the boys would hear the clicking sound of bicycle pedals but they knew that there was no-one about. Also wet seaweed would often be found on the front doorstep of the cottage in the mornings. It could not have been blown there as the cottage was about twenty yards from the beach and separated from it by a grassy bank.

The Ghosts That Haunt Greyabbey

Greyabbey is located in the Ards Peninsula. The abbey itself was established in 1193 by John de Courcy's wife Affreca for the Cistercian monks. De Courcy was an Anglo Norman Invader to this part of N. Ireland. It is said that she wanted the abbey built in thanksgiving for a safe landing after a very perilous sea journey.

There are two ghost stories related to the abbey. Firstly, if you visit the ruined abbey in the evenings, you may run the risk of bumping into a young male scholar who is seen carrying his books towards the door. He will be in quite a hurry as he enters the abbey. If you decide to follow him through the door, his figure will grow fainter and fainter until he disappears before your very eyes.

The second haunting involves a group of three ladies. They are the complete opposite of the scholar as they are very chatty, well dressed and life-like. They will also be seen walking towards the entrance. One could mistake them for being real until you look down and realise that they have no feet. They actually glide along on top of a mist.

The Ghosts That Haunt Greyabbey

Chapter 5
Banshees & Other Death Warnings

'Hast thou heard the Banshee at morn,
Passing by the silent lake,
Or walking the fields by the orchard?
Alas! that I do not rather behold
White garlands in the hall of my fathers.'

The Banshee mournful wails
In the midst of the silent, lonely, lonely night,
Plaining, she sings the song of death…

Ancient Irish Poem

Introduction

Of all the supernatural phenomena, the banshee is the single
one that is strongly associated with Ireland. The original
banshee (sidhe Bhean) or fairy woman was described as a
beautiful young girl from Tir Na nOg. Over the years her
appearance changed to that of an old hag with long hair
which she is seen combing. She appears as pale like a corpse
and covered in freckles and terrible eyes that stare at you with
great sadness because of the death that is going to occur. She
makes a mournful sound similar to a fox or a cat cry. The
keen (caoine) or funeral cry of the peasantry is said to be
an imitation of her cry. The banshee was sometimes called
'an bhean chaointe' which means the mourning woman.
There are also stories of banshees outside Ireland where Irish
families have settled in other countries. There are no male
banshees.

When more than one banshee comes to cry, the man or
woman who is dying must have been very holy or very brave.
Sometimes the banshee is accompanied by an immense black

coach, mounted by a coffin and drawn by headless horses. The banshee is also seen washing bloody clothing which is said to belong to the person whose death is near. Because of that she is also known as the 'washer woman'.

She wails as most people know, over the death of a member of some old Irish families especially those with 'Mc' or 'O' in their surnames. One of the most famous banshees in Irish Folk history was Aibhill who appeared to Brian Boro on the night before the Battle of Clontarf in 1014. Brian knew that he was soon to die.

River Bann Banshee Story

Many years ago, women used to bring their washing down to the River Bann after they had all their other chores done for the day. The women would meet up and walk as a group down to the River. This gave them the opportunity to catch up on the latest news or gossip in the area and also have a swim.

One such group of young girls were walking towards the river one summers evening when all of a sudden, a loud wailing sound was heard. Immediately, the girls became frightened at this noise as they realised it was the sound of the banshee. However, not everyone had heard the sound. One particular girl could not understand why the girls had become frightened. She could hear nothing at all.

The girls quickly continued to the river to get their washing completed and to get home as soon as possible. On the way back, the group were missing one girl- the one who had not heard the banshee. They searched for her but to no avail and decided eventually that she must have gone on ahead.

However, she had not returned home. When the other girls recited their story, neighbours became very anxious. They told the group that whoever does not hear the banshee will become its next victim and will die very soon. Unfortunately, their friend's body was discovered the next day where she had drowned in the River Bann.

The River Bann

Banshee Story From Barr

Once a man set out to visit his father who he had just heard was very ill. A banshee followed him the whole way as he travelled through the countryside on route to his father's house in Barr. This was a very frightening companion and the man became very anxious about his father and wanted to get there as soon as possible. His fears came through true as when he reached the house, his family members told him that his father had died.

Newcastle Harbour Banshee Tale

A banshee is supposed to haunt Newcastle Harbour and has been seen walking among the tied up boats and lobster pots. She has been heard crying out in a high pitched voice. This is seen as a warning to the boatmen not to go out to sea as an impending death is imminent.

"He had many strange sights to keep him cheerful or to make him sad. I asked him had he ever seen the faeries, and got the reply, 'Am I not annoyed with them?' I asked too if he had ever seen the banshee. 'I have seen it,' he said, 'down there by the water, batting the river with its hands.'

("A Teller of Tales") by Yeats. From The Celtic Twilight: Faerie and Folklore

Floating Coffins in Attical

It is claimed that some families in Attical, outside Kilkeel, have an amazing gift of seeing into the future. However, that gift is one that can actually foretell the death of a person. To some readers, this is a burdensome gift and not one that everyone would want.

Their amazing powers involve seeing coffins floating in the night sky. At the house where the coffins stop and revolve to rest in an upright position, will indicate that someone who lives there will die very soon.

One family member can recall seeing two coffins floating in the sky one clear winter's night. The coffins stopped outside a house quite close to where he was standing. The coffins then turned upright. The story teller was puzzled by this event as there was no-one living in the house, the family had emigrated to Australia some years before. However, two months later word came through that two members of the family who had moved away had passed away. They were involved in a tragic drowning accident that had actually occurred on the same date that the coffins were seen hovering over their old Attical home.

Floating Coffins in Attical

The Wee Woman of the Knock

The Knockiveagh is widely known as being as a Neolithic site and dates back nearly 3000 years.

Late in the winter of 2013 a woman and her child were travelling along the Iveagh road near the Knock hill. The woman had just been coming back from collecting her daughter from school in Annaclone. It was approximately

3.30 in the afternoon. As they travelling along the road they noticed a girl coming towards them on a horse. They pulled their car into a lane way and turned the engine off to allow the horse and its rider to go past. However, as they did this the child said to her mother *"do you see that wee lady standing in the middle of the road?"* The woman replied that she did not see anyone! The mother assured the little girl that there was no one there but she was adamant there was. As the horse approached the spot on the road where the child claimed to see the little woman the horse suddenly jumped into the air. It stood up on its back legs forcing its rider to hold on for their life. The horse refused to go any further and was trembling with fear. It had also noticed something on the road. The rider turned the horse around in an effort to try and settle it down. After a few minutes the horse calmed down again and the girl coaxed it along slowly. However, once the horse reached the same spot in the road again it had the exact same reaction. Just as this happened the child said to its mother *"Look did you see that mum, the wee woman ran into the hedge?"* *"No, I didn't, there is nothing there!"* replied the mother.

The Iveagh road is quite narrow with little room to pass another vehicle so the horse rider wanted to let the car go past as they had been waiting for quite a while. The rider tried a third time to walk up the road but the horse absolutely refused. There was no other alternative for the girl but to turn the horse around and go back the same way they had come. Meanwhile the woman in the car was starting to think that maybe her daughter was telling the truth and there was something or someone on the road after seeing the reaction of the horse. She decided to take a closer look at the area where the horse was spooked. Sometimes even a plastic bag or something in the hedge could frighten a horse but the woman could see that there was clearly nothing there. As they looked at the hedge the child said, *"Look mum, there's the hole where the woman ran into!"* The woman who the child saw was most likely to have been a banshee. This story helps prove the fact that some children and animals are more sensitive and can see ghosts and spirits whereas adults are more sceptical and see or sense nothing.

A view of the Knock Hill, Annaclone

Banshee at the End of the Bed, Annaclone

The townland of Tullintanvally in heart of Annaclone has been widely known for its ghost stories and many unexplained things have happened here over the years. There have been a huge number of banshee sightings and things associated with the fairies. This is most likely due to the fact that banshees are said to follow old Irish families and in particular surnames beginning with Mc or O.

One night two young brothers were in bed sleeping in a house near the Poland's bridge. During the night they were wakened by the sound of a woman crying and they could not understand what it was. They knew it was not their mother because they could hear her sleeping in the other room and the sound seemed to be coming from their room. One of them decided to get up and turn on the light to see who or what it was. As they switched on the light a small woman was seen standing at the end of their bed. They could both see her clearly and she was approximately 2-3feet tall. The boys were terrified as they thought it to be a ghost. One of them tried to shout for help but no words would come out of his mouth. The other one tried to hide under the sheets but he was completely frozen and could not move an inch. One of the boys who is now a man in his fifties described that it was as if his body was overcome with some sort of external force and he could not move at all no matter how hard he tried. After a few seconds though the woman disappeared right in front of their eyes.

Banshee at the End of the Bed, Annaclone

Chapter 6
Devil Related Stories

Squire Hawkin's Grave in Drumballyroney Graveyard

The Midnight Pact with Satan, East Down

Long ago in East Down, a retired army colonel lived in a great house with his wife and family. He was well known for his penny pinching ways and his love of all things gold. One Halloween night, when ghosts would begin their weary wander on earth, he decided to pray to the devil for more of the precious metal. After some time the room was filled with a putrid smell and when he looked up, he saw a young handsome, well dressed man. However, on looking down, he noticed that the man had cloven feet! At the end of that bewitched Halloween night, a dreadful pact had been made and signed in blood by both parties.

The agreement was that for the next twenty five years, the devil would agree to grant all the colonel's wishes but afterwards, the old man's body and soul would belong to him. Once agreed the devil vanished. The colonel began to think that the whole episode was merely a bad dream and he doubted that the agreement had indeed taken place. As a test, he decided to summon the devil once again and ordered him to fill up a nearby house with gold. Promptly agreeing, the devil climbed onto the roof and through a hole, he shovelled thousands of gold coins into the house. He stopped for a while and looked into the house and saw that the colonel had made a hole in the floor and all the gold was going into the foundations. He was very angry that the colonel was hiding the gold so that the devil would have to fill the house with even more gold.

Confronting the colonel, the devil warned, *"Learn once and for all"* he roared. *"Although I'm your servant, I'm not to be trifled with"*. He then instantly disappeared.

Many years past and the colonel lived happily off his hoard of gold. However, he and his wife were on very bad terms and they were always arguing and shouting at one another. After one particularly bad night of screaming at each other, the colonel decided on a final solution.

He summoned the devil once again and told him that he could no longer stand living with his wife. The devil knew what he had to do. One of the man's daughters was heard screaming upstairs and rushed down to tell her father that her mother had taken a violent seizure and was dying. Rushing upstairs, the man discovered that his wife had been strangled and lay dead on the bedroom floor. There were marks on her neck and her eyes bulged in terror.

The colonel was full of remorse when he realised what he had done and remained alone in his room for days on end, hardly eating. He even pleaded with the devil to return his wife back to life again but it was too late. The devil reminded him that he could not 'remove the stains from his soul'.

As the end of the twenty five years came closer, the colonel realised that the devil would be returning to claim his soul. He broke out in a cold sweat at the thought of it and wondered if there was any way out of the pact that he had foolishly entered into all those years ago. After a lot of thought, he thought of a plan and summoned the devil once again and commanded that he produce something that had never been made before. The devil was curious.

"I want you to make me a rope of sand!" the man laughed, thinking that he had outwitted the devil at last. If he could not make a rope of sand, then he could not claim the man's soul as he not fully served him for twenty five years.

The devil flew into a rage, shouting and swearing at the man and unbuckling his belt, he violently hit out at the man's face. The man felt an intense burning sensation in his eye as if hot sand had been poured into the socket. He cried in agony and realised that he was now blind in this eye. The devil laughed and disappeared again.

Halloween night was approaching fast and the colonel was in despair. He began to repent his evil ways and prayed to God for help. The fateful day arrived and the man was thin and pale with fear. Just as the day was finishing, the devil appeared ready to claim the doomed man's soul and asked if there if there were any final requests which he could grant. In desperation, the man thought of a plan and asked the devil to build him a brand new mill on his land and added that it must be finished that night.

After several hours the devil performed his final deed and the man could see the brand new mill. All the local people flocked to see the brand new building and the man took refuge inside.

As midnight drew closer, the devil confronted the old man, *"Your time has come"* he said. *"I have come to claim your soul!"* But as he went to grab him, the man held up the bible in front of him. The devil backed away. *"You cannot escape!"* mocked the devil. *"This is a journey we must both undertake!"* The colonel pleaded for his life and then cried out God's name as a last defence. The devil let out an unmerciful scream and suddenly vanished in a blaze of fire through a hole in the wall.

Satan's grip on the wretched old man was released at long last. For the rest of his life the old colonel remained a devout hermit and undertook penance for all his sins. He publicly declared his evil pact with Satan and what he had done and died peacefully a number of years later.

The mill itself stood for many years and became known as the Devil's Mill and still remains today though it is in ruins. This mill, built by unearthly forces can still be recognised. On one of the cornerstones, five long black fingers are burnt irremovably into the brickwork.

The Mystery of the Old Fox, Annaclone

Many years ago there used to be an old tramp who roamed the fields and roads around Annaclone. He was often described as having a long black and grey beard, a face which was black with soot from a fire and a long coat which was torn to shreds by him climbing over barbed wire fences.

He was nick-named the 'old fox' by the local people as he was cunning enough to turn up at people's houses just as they were sitting down for their tea. He would ask for any leftover food that could be spared. It was strange that he was rarely seen during the day. He was spied warming himself with a fire he had lit in a barrel at the side of a road or sometimes washing himself in the River Bann although he would become dirty again very soon after.

He did not appear to have any family or house of his own, nor any food or money to survive on. It was said that he ate wild rabbit and berries and also drank milk from cows in the fields around Annaclone. Many farmers noticed that their calves were quite thin as their cows did not have enough milk for them. But they would not say anything to him as they were scared that he would put a curse on them and their farms.

One particular lady named Hamilton who lived in Lisnasliggan in Annaclone would often give the old fox some food to eat. People thought that the old fox brought her a lot of luck as she happily lived to a very old age. Her son had previously left home at the age of eighteen to work in England but he recalled the tramp coming to his house when he was younger.

After his mother died, her son decided to return home to Ireland to live. When he arrived back in Annaclone, to his astonishment, the first person that he met was the old fox. He had not aged one bit and looked exactly as the son remembered him over fifty years previously. The old fox asked the son how his mother was keeping. The son replied that his mother had been dead for some time. *"I'm sorry to hear that"* the old fox said and added *"I would say she's happy!"*

After that encounter the old fox was never seen again in Annaclone. No one knows what happened to him but there are those that say he must have been a ghost, a fairy or even the devil himself!

The Mystery of the Old Fox, Annaclone

Shake Hands with the Devil, Rathfriland

Many years ago in Rathfriland there lived a man called Davey. He did not have a happy marriage and used to drink a lot of alcohol to drown his sorrows, blaming his misfortune on his wife.

One bright moonlit night as he was coming home from the local pub the worse for drink, he passed the local graveyard. As he looked over the wall, he leaned over too much and fell in to the graveyard. Just as he was getting to his feet, he saw a huge figure over seven feet tall standing in front of him. The figure asked him, *"Do you want to shake hands with the Devil?"* Davey gathered himself and replied very sincerely, *"Would you like to shake hands with the man who married his daughter?"*

Hell's Fire is Your lot, A Leitrim Story

In the 1800s there once existed a small hill farm in Leitrim that seemed to be cursed as no crops would grow on it.

A young widow eventually purchased the farm with the intention of making a living out of it for her and her young child. Local people were puzzled by this especially as she had little or no farming experience and she was often ridiculed as she passed by her neighbours.

The following spring was very wet and brought disaster to many farmers as their crops were destroyed and potatoes blighted. However, for some strange reason, all was well on the widow's farm with lush green grass and crops. One neighbouring farmer decided to visit the widow to congratulate her. He set out on a very wet summer's day but as he approached her cottage the sun was shining, yet when he looked back all he saw were dark clouds and skies.

No-one appeared to be at home and as he was about to walk away, he overheard a voice. Looking through one of the windows, he caught sight of the young widow inside asking for many requests as she read from a large black book. He knocked on the door and was invited to enter inside. Asking for a drink of milk to distract the widow, he managed to look at the book which was in another room. On the book's front cover was the words 'READ ME ALL THROUGH BUT PRACTICE ME NOT, FOR IF YOU DO HELL'S FIRE IS YOUR LOT'.

He quickly returned to the front room to wait for his milk and looked through a small crack in a door at his host who was in the scullery. She had stuck a fork into a table and milk was pouring out of the holes and into a glass. On observing this strange sight, the farmer quickly left the cottage and hurried straight to the parish priest to relate his story.

A few hours later, the priest decided to call at the widow's home for himself. Just as he was half way up the lane, his horse went crazy and he fell off. Shaking and bruised, the priest continued on his way to the cottage on foot. The door opened as he came nearer and he could see the widow inside shouting *"Leave this house! Leave this house!"*

The priest held firm and implored the young widow to destroy the book and never to read from it again.

Immediately the front door slammed shut and the cottage burst into flames! Helpless, the priest watched as it was completely destroyed. All the lush green grass turned to rushes and it started to rain once again on the farm. Neighbours rushed to the farm when they saw the flames but there was no sign of the bodies of the widow or her child. All that remained was the large black book and it remained intact and undamaged by the fire.

One neighbour carefully wrapped the book in a cloth and buried it under an old oak tree, where, to this day, it remains buried and not to be disturbed.

The mystery of the hill farm and the book has never been explained. Some say that the widow had been once visited by a man dressed in black who promised her a good life as long as he could have her soul in return. Who was this mysterious man? Some say it was the Devil himself.

Hawkin's Ghost

Squire Hawkins, whose grave lies in the Drumballyroney Church graveyards, was reputedly one of the founder members of the Rathfriland Hell-Fire Club. The Hell-Fire Club was one of a number throughout Ireland and England during the 18th and 19th centuries. Its members were often misguided men or 'rakes' of that time who were only interested in partying, immoral activities, debauchery, the Black Art and also devil worship. There is no evidence of any such devil worship in the Rathfriland branch where they held their meetings in the cellar of the former Clanwilliam Arms in the Square.

When the wealthy Hawkins died, his coffin was carried on the back of a horse-drawn carriage from Rathfriland to Ballyroney with his family and servants walking behind. On reaching the gates of the churchyard, the black horses reared up and foamed at the mouth. Despite the efforts of the servants, the horses refused to enter into the graveyard. They were whipped and pulled back and forward, this way and that but nothing could get them to go through the gates. Eventually, the Squire's coffin had to be lifted from the hearse and carried through the gates to his grave where it was lowered and covered over with soil.

Later that night, while everyone was sleeping soundly they were awakened by one of the most ferocious storms to hit the town of Rathfriland. Some people said that this as the noise of the devil as he came to claim the Squire's soul for himself! The next day some family members came to check on Squire Hawkins grave. They could not believe their eyes.

Sometime, during the thunderstorm of the previous night, the family tombstone had been struck by lightning and there was the sign of the cross formed on the stone. Everyone was convinced that this was God's way of getting his revenge on the Squire as he had not believed in his existence during his life. This cross was a warning it was said from God himself not to dabble with the forces of darkness.

Another story involved a man walking home from Rathfriland after attending the Hell-Fire Club. He journeyed down the 'Bann Hill' when all of a sudden he heard what sounded like footsteps behind him. He assumed that these were coming from another traveller who was also making his way home. The footsteps got louder and louder until they sounded more like hooves as if someone was approaching on horseback. The man turned around, expecting to see a horse and its rider but what he actually saw was a more monstrous figure.

It was the hideous spectre of the figure of a man with horns on his head, the face of a ghost and instead of feet it had cloven hooves: it was the Devil himself!

The man was so frightened that he started to run for his life and said the Lord's Prayer as he did so. Ever after that incident, he refused to walk home again alone and he never returned to the Hell-Fire Club.

A Dance with the Devil, Hilltown Hall

During the 1970s a group of young girls travelled from Rostrevor to a dance in the INF Hall in Hilltown. It was the 'in' place at the time for ceilidhs and country and western dances and many young people travelled there from far and wide. Boys and girls would attend in the hope of finding a new partner and because there were people from all over the country there, there were lots of new faces each night.

One of the Rostrevor girls spotted this handsome young fella from across the dance floor and she admitted to her friends that she would love to dance with him. He was tall, cleanly shaven and had long brown hair. The others spitefully remarked that she would stand no chance and he was unlikely to look twice at her. However, she noticed him looking around the hall and his eyes met hers and he stared at her for a while before smiling back. Moments later he moved towards the girl and taking her hand he asked her for a dance. Her friends could not believe her luck as he was the best looking man there. The couple never left the dance floor all night and were getting on a like a house on fire. The girl was starting to think that she had met her future husband.

Eventually the music stopped at one o'clock and the couple left the hall together. They decided to go to the local chippy at the bottom of the street for some food before they went home. As they walked hand in hand down the street, the girl glanced down at her companion's feet and realised that he was not wearing any shoes and in fact he had hoofed or clubbed feet.

Terrified, she ran off as fast as she could to get away from him. She had realised that the man of her dreams was in fact the 'devil' himself. Her screams could be heard all over Hilltown. Her friends had seen her panic and were able to describe how the young man simply disappeared before their very eyes and could not be found anywhere. Their friend was traumatised for a long time after that encounter.

A Dance with the Devil, Hilltown Hall

Chapter 7
Witch Hare Stories

Introduction

The Irish Hare was a symbolic animal and was found on the old Irish three pence piece. In Ireland the hare was believed to be a witch in disguise. This belief may have arisen from an earlier religious meaning for the hare which was mythically connected to the 'Cailleach', a witch-like being. Caesar is said to have written that it was taboo for the Celts to eat the flesh of the hare as it was a sacred animal. It was said that eating a hare was like eating one's own grandmother due to the sacred connection between hares and the various Celtic goddesses and warrior queens. The Celtic Goddess Eostre's favourite animal was the hare and it was claimed that she used to change into a hare at each full moon.

There was a belief that witches could transform themselves into hares. Old widows or spinsters were often blamed for farmers' misfortunes. When a hare was injured it was noticed that a nearby old woman would also have the same type of injury and it was therefore claimed that she was in fact a witch. If one discovered a group of hares, it was believed that it was actually a witches' coven. The only way to kill a hare was to use a silver bullet or a crooked sixpence piece.

Several years ago a hare was killed and it was discovered that there was a pin sunk deep into the flesh of one of its hind legs. People believed that the pin would have come from the witch's apron when she was flying through the air. In the other hind leg a fly hook was found leading to the belief that the hare was once flying over the sea on a broomstick or sailing through the sea inside a mussel shell. There are many stories concerning the witch hare, a hare who could never be caught and who used to drink all the milk from the cows before morning. People referred to such cows as having been 'blinked'. One such case happened in Knockanerney, Donaghmore.

A local farmer wanted to hunt down a hare which had been seen near his cows. Accompanied by his hounds, he went out one day to hunt for the hare. The hounds found it and chased it past the door of a nearby cottage. In the cottage lived an old woman, her daughter and grandchildren. One of the young children was standing in the doorway and just as the hare ran past, the farmer could hear the child shout out, *"Run, Granny! Run"!*

A Witch Hare

The Witch Of Warrenpoint

Along the Clonallen Road in Warrenpoint lies the Hill of Black Jenny. Jenny was the name of a local witch who once lived there. It is said that she used to sit inside her cabin at her spinning wheel and weave many spells and charms. Like all witches, Jenny had a black cat and the story goes that the cat used to speak to Jenny. Once the cat was overheard asking Jenny *"Jenny, where's the broomstick?"*

Visitors to the witch's cabin were often frightened at hearing the cat speak and many a visitor actually fainted on the spot!

Black Jenny was also said to appear in frightening shapes and play tricks on travellers in the area. One dark night two local farmers saw her dismount from her broomstick. Her appearance frightened their horses and they bolted off down the hill causing the men to fall off and they were killed in the process. It was said that she often turned into a hare and milked the poor farmers' cows before the people were up in the mornings.

Eventually the local people summoned up enough courage and they went to the Authorities and accused Black Jenny of sorcery, making the butter leave the churn, the cows to go dry, rotting the potatoes in the ground and of assuming dreadful shapes to frighten passers-by. She was arrested and brought before a special court.

During the court case, Jenny refused to speak and accordingly she was found guilty. She was sentenced to death and was taken back to the hill and was burned at the stake. It is said that her ghost still haunts the hill in the form of a white hare.

A view of Warrenpoint

The Witch - Hare

This is a true story which was told by the writer's grandfather about an old-woman-witch, who lived up the Roosley mountain. In the evening she would change herself into a hare, and the farmers became very angry, for different reasons, as you'll read in the poem. These happenings supposedly took place in the eighteenth century.

In the early eighteenth century,

This my mother related to me,

About this wee old woman, who changed,

At the on-set of the dew,

She'd change herself into a hare,

As across the fields, she flew,

Now, the farmers, they assembled,

To see what they could do.

She'd make her way into a byre,

And suck the milkin' cow,

Well, this went on for too long,

She'd have to go, somehow.

One evening, as this farmer prepared,

The milkin' to be done,

Headed 'round beyond the cow-shed,

At the settin' of the sun,

As soon as he reached the byre door,

This hare, she did charge out,

And, across the fields she sprinted,

Then, a single shot rang out.

For, hidin' low behind a ditch,

A young farmer was lurking there,

He vowed the last thing that he'd do,

Was to catch this flamin' hare.

She changed her course, and back she came,

To pass close by the byre,

And left a tiny trail of blood,

As she began to tire.

Then, hid herself in the bracken,

Along the loanin's trail,

And, all that night, some neighbours said,

They heard her lonely wail.

Next mornin' the old woman was seen,

A-limpin' round the field,

The early dew upon the grass,

Would help her wound to heal.

Well, someone got the doctor,

For, they knew she was in pain,

But, she stole down by the river,

And was never seen again.

By Alice Kelly

Witch Hare near Tandragee

Another story concerns two brothers who could not get any butter to form from their cow's milk. They suspected that an old neighbour woman had 'blinked' the cows so one of the brothers decided to lie in wait with his shotgun.

Knowing that an ordinary lead bullet was useless, he melted down a silver coin and shaped it into a special bullet for the purpose. Sure enough the hare appeared and the farmer shot it. He only managed to injure its leg and it ran quickly away. The next day the old woman was seen out but she was hobbling and had to use a walking stick as she had injured her leg.

Chapter 8

Other Mysteries & Unusual Stories

The Disappearance of Audleystown

Audleystown was a small settlement of cottages located in the grounds of Castleward on Strangford Lough. Castleward was occupied by Viscount Bangor and his wife Harriet. After the Viscount died, Lady Bangor married Major Andrew Nugent. It was decided to get rid of the cottages as part of estate improvements, although some people have said that Lady Bangor just did not like the look of the poor cottages which spoilt her view of the Lough. They were all demolished and all twenty five or so families who lived there were evicted. They were also forced to agree to deportation from Strangford Quay to Boston in America to start a new life.

So on 28th October 1852 all the former Audleystown residents boarded a ship called 'The Rose' for their journey across the Atlantic. This journey would have taken three months but nothing was ever heard of the families after they set sail. No descendants of the families have ever appeared in America: the families all seem to have disappeared. No-one knows where the families ended up, if the ship was lost at sea or worse still were the passengers thrown overboard at the hands of the ruthless captain under instructions from their previous landlord?

The original rent book from 1852 details the names of the twenty five families.

Surnames included Lowry, Johnston, Orr, Quigley, Hinds, Skillen, Swail, Mahon, Matthews, Quinn, Power, Coffey, Vint, O'Connell, O'Brier, Taylor, Doolan, O'Faolain, Smyth, Pearse, O'Malley and Quilligan.

The disappearance of these families has remained a mystery since they left the shores of Strangford Lough. All that remains of the original settlement are some overgrown steps.

County Down Centenarians

It is common knowledge that people are now living longer. So it is surprising to discover so many centenarians in County Down from the 19th and early 20th centuries.

In 1898, several UK newspapers recorded the death of the 'Queens's Oldest Subject' and 'probably the oldest man in the world'. He was Robert Taylor, a former sub postmaster from Scarva who was aged about 119 years of age. He once marched as a piper at the head of his yeomanry regiment from Scarva to County Dublin during the 1798 Rebellion. Queen Victoria sent him a framed photograph of herself as a gift.

Another centenarian was Catherine McAfee from Rathfriland who died at the age of 115 years of age in 1903. She left behind a total of eighty three male descendants including sons, grandsons, great grandsons and sons-in-law all following the occupation of shoemakers.

In 1892, the Dundee Courier reported the funeral of William Gamble at Tullylish. He was aged 103 and was a farm labourer. The Aberdeen Journal reported the death of Mary O'Hara in 1906. She was aged 106 and lived outside Castlewellan.

Bridget Sheridan from Kilcoo died at the remarkable age of 115 years in 1897. She was a hawker and worked at this until just before her death. She was also known for her very good memory.

William McCrory of Hunter Street, Belfast died in 1927 at the age of 107 years. It was reported that he was probably the oldest man in the United Kingdom when he died. He attributed his long life to a simple diet including porridge, oaten bread and raw vegetables. He worked until the age of 99 years.

John Byrne from Glascar died at the age of 110 years in December 1894. He was a farmer and had lived there all his life and had been able to walk about up to his last few days. Another nearby centenarian was Hugh Fraser, a farmer from Edenagarry who died just after reaching his one hundredth birthday.

Mrs Hannah Barclay died in Ballynahinch in 1929 at the age of 106 years and was reported to have been able to recite a Psalm from memory only a few days previously.

Margaret Kerr from Aughnavallog, Ballyroney died at the age of 102 in 1920. She had lived for the whole of her life on one farm and never had an illness until a few days before her death.

Daughter Disappears in Katesbridge

In 1868, an article appeared in the Newry Reporter and was widely reported in other newspapers throughout the rest of the United Kingdom including The Dundee Courier and The Cheshire Observer.

The story concerns the daughter of a farmer who was seeing a neighbouring farmer's son. Her parents were not happy about the liaison and the girl was often chastised and on one occasion was even sent away from home as a punishment for her continued involvement with the young man.

On another occasion the pair was discovered together again and the girl was dragged back to her home and beaten. She managed to escape but was forced back into the house by her parents. On this occasion, neighbours could hear her screaming and even though they tried, they could not get into the house to help her. Eventually they managed to break down the door and found a rope with a noose on its end suspended from the ceiling. But there was no sign of the farmer's daughter.

At school the next day her younger brothers and sisters claimed that their sister had been hung up by her parents and then carried away. The local constabulary were informed of the whole incident. Although they investigated her disappearance, the girl was never seen again and her parents denied any knowledge of her whereabouts.

Without the evidence of a body, the police could do nothing and they never discovered the true events surrounding her disappearance. No-one knows what really happened to the poor girl all those years ago.

Severe Weather

Our weather is very unpredictable and many relate this to Climate Change. It is interesting to note that severe weather conditions prevailed in the 19th and early 20th centuries.

A drought in Ireland was reported in August 1887. The extensive bleach works at Greenvale near Castlewellan belonging to Messrs Murland were closed on 23rd August for an indefinite period owing to the continued drought. Hundreds of hands were laid off with the newspaper predicting how 'serious distress, will it is feared, ensue'.

Nine years previously in 1878, a terrible thunderstorm swept over Newry and the surrounding area one morning. Heavy rain, thunder and lightning lasted for over two hours. The storm resulted in two deaths one on the Warrenpoint Road and the other was a fowl dealer from Loughbrickland. During the following year, the rainfall around Rathfriland was exceptional causing some parts of roads to be swept away. In Hilltown, the house of farmer Peter Clark was struck by lightning and a hole was torn in the roof resulting in the tragic death of one of his young sons who was sleeping below.

More gales, storms and floods were reported throughout Ireland in 1901with serious damage caused throughout Ulster. In the Newry Area, rivers overflowed, flooding low lying areas. Many houses in Newry were flooded and their occupants were imprisoned in the upper rooms. Several spinning mills had to cease work and the Great Northern Railway Station was entirely submerged. Several houses in Bangor were blown down and the Lagan burst its banks in Lisburn. In Tandragee, the lake inside the Duke of Manchester's demesne burst its banks and the rush of water caused a boundary wall to collapse. A workman called Ferris was trapped underneath and he was crushed to death.

In March 1905 a terrible storm raged in the Newry District with the force of the wind smashing windows and street lamps. In the country areas stacks of corn and hay were destroyed, trees blown down and many lambs perished in the severe conditions.

It rained ink in Castlewellan in May 1885! It was reported that a heavy fall of blood red hail fell in the town and when local residents squeezed the ice pellets, their fingers became deeply stained red.

A Banbridge Romance

This story was printed in America in 1902 and involved 'Harry Warren who will be returning from Ireland next month with his bride, a woman who has been waiting for twenty years'. The name of his new bride was Maria Thompson from Banbridge.

It went on to explain that Mr Warren had attended Trinity College in Dublin where his father was a wealthy banker. He had met Miss Thompson and they got engaged. Suddenly Henry's father died and after his estate was settled, it was discovered that his father had accumulated many debts.

Henry vowed that he would not marry his fiancée until all the debts were cleared and he offered Maria her freedom from the engagement. However Maria said that she would wait for him no matter how long it would take.

After some years Henry managed to clear all the debts and although he had not corresponded with Maria he knew that she was still living. He decided to send her a telegram cable.

'*All debts paid. I am coming*'. She replied, '*I am waiting*'. Mr Warren is now making his way over to Ireland.

The Proposal Stones of the Mournes

Proposal Stones were rectangular shaped rocks on which lovers sat and whispered sweet nothings to each other. They almost always overlooked fairy forts or were located close to a fairy tree. Hundreds of years ago they were common-place throughout Ireland when folklore and fairy stories were popular in the lives of people.

The couple who sat on the stone made a wish for long happiness together and hoped that the fairies would bring them luck and also watch over them for the rest of their lives. A tradition arose where marriage proposals were not considered seriously unless the lady concerned was seated on one of the stones. In fact couples returned to the stones to renew their love for one another with the man asking the lady if she would do it all over again if he was to ask for her hand in marriage. If the lady answered yes without hesitation the fairies would then heap more luck on their relationship.

By the early 19th century, the church became alarmed at the superstitions relating to the proposal stones and had many of the stones moved closer to churches and monasteries. Lovers were synonymous with sin in the eyes of the clergy back then and couples were not prepared to be caught and risk public denouncement and damnation. This action deterred the ardent lovers and couples from using the stones and their popularity fell and their strange powers started to be forgotten about.

The stones themselves began to disappear and were lost when ditches or houses were being built. Some isolated stones however, do survive in a few parts of Ireland. One such location is at the Ghan Road in Carlingford, County Louth and the stones there are reputed to have come from the Fairy Glen in Rostrevor, County Down. In 2012, these Proposal Stones were used once again when the bride to be said yes to a proposal of marriage and the happy couple signed a book located in a chest close to the stones.

The Proposal Stones of the Mournes

There's Gold in Them There Hills

At a meeting of the Royal Irish Society of Antiquarians it was announced that a gold mine had been discovered in Ballyroney, County Down. The yield from the stones was two ounces of gold to the ton.

Other strange finds in the county include a huge oyster in Warrenpoint in 1895. It was claimed to have been one of the biggest found in the past fifty years. It measured twenty one inches in circumference and weighed thirty five ounces. Experts believed that the oyster was over sixty years old.

According to a newspaper in October 1890, an important find of petroleum was discovered on a farm in the Estate of the Earl of Kilmorey in Moneydarragh near Kilkeel. A sample was sent to Dublin for analysis.

In 1874, it was reported that an Iron Ore deposit discovered in Dechomet was now employing up to sixty men. The ore was transported to Dundrum for export.

My Little Black Dog, Burren

This is story from the 1800s. An elderly unmarried Burren lady lived alone and her only friend was her little black dog. The woman was called Jane and she never went anywhere without her little dog. Before she retired to bed, the dog would lie beside the fire with her and when she went to bed, the dog slept underneath her bed. When Jane put her hand down the side of the bed, the dog would lick her hand. This reassured Jane.

One dark wet night, Jane had read about a dangerous murderer who had escaped prison and who was on the run. He was known for murdering woman who lived alone. With that chilling thought in mind, Jane retired to bed and tried to sleep. She tossed and turned for ages and then reached down to where her dog usually lay. A warm wet tongue licked her hand and she felt safe once again. However, she opened her eyes for a moment and saw that her little black dog was actually across the room in front of the fireplace. You can only imagine who was under her bed!

My Little Black Dog, Burren

'Gypsy's Curse', Banbridge

In the 1800s, many Irish Traveller families travelled the length and breadth of Ireland, camping outside towns and villages while the men would seek work locally. One such family would camp outside Banbridge in a wooden glen owned by one the larger mill owners.

For many years the Travellers kept themselves to themselves and they got on very well with the mill owner. This all changed one particular summer when the mill owner's son took advantage of one of the young Traveller girls. Her father was very angry and went to see the mill owner himself. However, the mill owner just laughed and dismissed the whole affair. In retaliation, the girl's father placed a 'gypsy curse' on the mill owner's family.

His curse involved the future violent death of his sons and also that the common people of the area, who he looked down his nose at, would run through his land and erect many houses. Many say that the curse did come true as the mill owner's estate was sold and today the land is occupied by houses. Other strange happenings have occurred over the years in the vicinity of his former house which still stands to this day.

Watch the Gravediggers in Kilcoo

This story came from Moyadd in Kilcoo in 1927. When a local farmer died, his two neighbours set off to dig a grave for him taking a bottle of whiskey and a dozen Guinness. To give themselves some strength, they decided to have a drink before they started their task.

Some hours later, the funeral cortege arrived at the church and the undertaker went to the graveyard to check on the status of the new grave. But no new grave was dug and the two neighbours were found lying drunk and sleeping behind the cemetery wall!

Other Kilcoo Tales

In 1930 in Moyadd, old Tom Finney died. It was a very cold winter's day in March with at least six inches of snow on the ground. The Minister had to walk from Ballyroney to Kilcoo to pray over Tom's remains. As he entered the house, he was shivering and commented "*Poor old Tom. There's no snow where you are today!*"

Carnivals used to be held in Kilcoo many years ago with the latest county and western show bands appearing. It was custom for local men to look after the huge rented tent during the night to make sure nothing happened to it after each dance. Just before sunrise, one of the helpers was making his way home after a long night but did not know that two of his colleagues were about to play a trick on him. They had hurried on in front of him and hid in the local graveyard as he approached. Covering themselves in sheets, they jumped out on the unsuspecting man and frightened the life out of him. He ran off as quickly as he could. Later that morning, it was noticed that his 'smalls' were hanging out on his clothes line.

Wise Headstone, Bryansford

One particular headstone has the following inscription

'REMEMBER FRIENDS AS YOU PASS BY AS YOU ARE NOW SO ONCE WAS I, AS I AM NOW SO SOON YOU SHALL BE, SO PREPARE YOURSELF FOR DEATH AND FOLLOW ME"

Strange Parcel, Belfast

In 1883, the Dundee Courier reported this strange story which occurred in Belfast. An Edinburgh man called Porteous appeared in Court in Belfast. He had been charged with putting his three week old daughter into a hamper and despatching the hamper by train to Coleraine. This event occurred during a cold November day in 1882. The prisoner was remanded. Luckily the little child survived her ordeal.

Mother's Strange Dream, Belfast

In 1907, a young boy was abducted and was missing for

several days. Luckily he was found gagged and bound in an empty house in the city. As the boy recovered, he was unable to speak as his throat had been injured. His mother prayed very hard to God to reveal to her who had subjected her young son to such a hideous experience. She had the same dream three times in succession about a particular person and then strangely, when her son was able to talk, he also incriminated the same person. All this information was given to the Police at the time.

Rabies Scare, Castlewellan.

In 1889, it was reported that nine dogs were shot in Castlewellan. This was caused by a stray dog, which was believed to be rabid, as it passed through the streets of the town and worried eight other local dogs. The local District Inspector followed the dog and shot it while the 'other brutes' were promptly disposed of in a similar manner by other police officers.

Prize Cow, Ballybrick

In 1853, Matthew McClure from Ballybrick, a tenant of William Sharman Crawford Esq. sold a cow which was allegedly 32years old. The cow had given birth to 27 Bull calves and during the previous winter had produced 5/6 quarts of milk daily. This particular cow was of an old Irish Breed.

Revenge of the Mourne Dog

Life was very hard for hill farmers in County Down in the 19th Century and money was hard to find. Such farmers relied on their sheep dogs to help around the farm and normally they were treasured animals and were never subject to cruelty. However one particular farmer in the Mournes, who managed a small hill farm, was well known in the area for being very bad tempered. He took his temper out on his wife and family but also his poor dog. When the farmer died, few people were sorry and fewer still attended his funeral.

As the grave digger filled in the grave after the funeral sermon, he thought he heard noises coming from the coffin. He examined closer and saw the deceased farmer's dog 'peeing' over his former master's coffin. The grave digger chuckled at this scene and believing that it was the dog making the noise, he continued filling up the grave.

About four years later, the farmer's wife passed away. Once again the grave was opened to prepare for her burial. The grave digger noticed that the lid of the farmer's coffin was broken and he could see scratch marks inside! He then remembered the noises he had heard years before when he had been covering that same coffin with soil.

Word went round the district about the broken coffin. Neighbours wondered if the farmer had come round in his coffin and had been trying to get out. Eventually they concluded that the farmer's dog had eventually got its revenge on his cruel master. Some said that noises could be heard from that same grave for years to come on the anniversary of the farmer's death.

St. Patrick's Altar Stone

An ancient altar stone used to lie in the ruins of the abbey at Saul. It was over ten feet long and was said to have been used by St. Patrick to celebrate Holy Communion.

In 1757, a Downpatrick man ordered the stone to be taken to his new house and used as a step. As the cart left the abbey with its load, the oxen started to act very strangely and overturned the cart breaking the large stone. Many misfortunes affected the man who had wanted the stone and he died a broken man. As for the stone, it was moved to Saul Chapel and it still lies in its broken condition in this church.

The 'Crying Boy' Painting - A Curse or Something Else?

Let me first disclose that I, Sean, am from County Down and am the proud owner of one of the original prints of 'The Crying Boy' signed by Bragolin (Giovanni Bragolin was the pseudonym of the Spanish painter Bruno Amadio). When I was a small boy, I remember such a painting hanging over the fireplace in the family home and it now has pride of place in my own home accompanied by his little female friend/sister! Both of these paintings were extremely popular household decorations during that period.

In the early 1980s, British fire fighters noticed a strange phenomenon when they were attending to house fires. They began to observe that although most items were badly burned or charred, paintings of the wide-eyed sorrowful boy with a tear running down each cheek had not even a scorch mark on them. An article appeared in the Sun Newspaper in 1985 when fireman Peter Hall described these eerie events. After the publication, the newspaper's telephone lines were flooded with people relating their own experiences and where in many instances, their homes had burned down sometime after acquiring the Crying Boy painting. Some claimed that the painting was jinxed and one lady claimed that she had unsuccessfully tried to burn the painting.

Numerous tales explaining why the boy was crying began to emerge. Some said that the painter mistreated the boy who was an orphan, others said that the boy had set the fires as his own parents had previously died in a house fire and he was once again acting out the trauma. Psychics theorised that the boy's spirit was trapped in the painting. Others claimed that if the painting was hung up beside that of the sister painting of the young girl then there would be no problems.

The widespread anxiety that all these stories generated resulted in the editor of the Sun, Kelvin MacKenzie to actually inform his readers 'Enough is enough, folks. If you are worried about the Crying Boy picture hanging in your home, send it to us immediately. We will destroy it for you and that should be the end of the curse….' The 31st October edition of the Sun reported that 2,500 copies of the painting were burned under the supervision of the fire brigade.

Mackenzie would not allow one copy of the painting to be hung in any of the Sun's offices.

Luckily the painting remained in my parent's house and I maintained a special bond with the Crying Boy as I grew up. Years later, I became a joiner and started to work in Belfast. One particular day, in the tea hut, one of the other workers, who was from Longford, started to talk about the Crying Boy picture. He added that if one found the print of the Crying Girl by the same artist and hung them together, the curse would be lifted. Years later, I found and purchased that picture in the Car Boot Sale in Dundrum. The old painting cost me three pounds and I hurried home and immediately began to look for two new frames as my parents had given me their painting of the boy. As the two paintings hang in my living room, there is a feeling of safety and contentment. I believe that there is a lot of hidden power in the boy's eyes and a feeling of unspoken communication and bonding between myself and the painting. As I value these two paintings so much, I will stipulate in my will that they be bequeathed to someone who will keep them together, treat them with respect and never allow them to be separated.

Finally, research has revealed that the model of the boy was a street urchin found by the artist in Madrid in 1969. Bragolin was touched by his sorrowful look and he painted the boy. A Catholic priest identified him as Don Bonillo, a child who had run away after seeing his parents die in a fire. The priest advised Bragolin to have nothing to do with the street urchin as he had heard that wherever he settled, fires would mysteriously break out. However, Bragolin ignored the advice and adopted the boy. The portrait sold very well. One day unfortunately the artist's studio went on fire and the angrily, Bragolin accused the boy of arson. Bonillo ran off in tears and was never seen again.

The same researcher then discovered the following information. In 1976, a very bad car crash occurred where the car actually exploded into a fireball on the outskirts of Barcelona after crashing into a wall. The victim's body was charred beyond recognition, but part of his driving licence was found in the glove compartment and it was only partly burned. The name on the licence was that of 19 year old Don Bonillo. (Reference – The Curse of the Crying Boy Paintings by Valerie Ferrari)

The 'Crying Boy' Painting

Chapter 9
Ancient Myths & Legends

The Piastha, Mayobridge

This story concerns the Lake Dragon, a Guardian of hidden treasure and the Bo-Men Fairies who live in the marshes of County Down.

In the marshes near Mayobridge, they say that these creatures guard a treasure buried on an ancient cave below a Fort.

The only time a human is permitted to enter the cave is on a certain night in November provided he/she knows the secret password. Any human who is unlucky to be caught by the Bo-Men fairies will have a curse put on them which lasts for over ten years!

This actual story originates from one such unlucky Mayobridge person who we will call Seamus. He was cursed for ten years way back in the 1890s.

Saint Bronach's Bell, Rostrevor

Many hundreds of years ago County Down was ruled by the local chieftains. One such chieftain was Fergus of Glenn Secis. One day he was out hunting red deer in the Mourne Mountains near the Deer's Meadow. He and his men came across a mighty stag which he resolved to capture with the help of his two favourite hounds. Fergus ventured out on his own to accomplish this task and when he caught up with the stag, he was surprised to see a rival chieftain, Artan of Lecale also pursuing the same deer.

As the dogs attacked the stag, one of Artan's hounds was gored to death by its sharp antlers. Artan was dismayed and annoyed on losing his best hound and he fired his javelin at the stag but instead killed the hound of Fergus. This in turn enraged Fergus and thinking Artan's act was done deliberately, he shot an arrow at Artan hitting him on the chest.

Grief stricken, Fergus carried his dead hound home. As time passed by, he started to become nervous and irritable and feared a war would evolve between his and Artan's Clan. Fergus became very religious and commissioned a bell and twelve bronze candlesticks and presented them to Saint Bronach and her religious community in Rostrevor. Bronach placed the bell in a recess in an oak tree near her church.

Fergus still was not happy and decided to leave his chieftaincy and as a further act of atonement, he dressed himself in sack cloth and sandals and left the area completely to travel as a pilgrim through many lands far away. After almost fifty years of penance, he decided to return home.

On his return he found his homeland ravaged by the Danes and the convent and church in ruins. He came across an old man near the church and he enquired what had happened. During the conversation Fergus realised that he was actually talking to Artan of Lecale who he had thought he had killed all those many years ago.

Artan explained that he had only been injured but even though he lay ill for many weeks, he survived. Fergus's heart swelled with gratitude and the weight of his life burden was lifted off him. Suddenly a breeze shook the trees and the old bell rang out. Fergus started to tremble and he fell on his knees begging Artan to forgive him. Fergus then fell forward and died in the arms of his old enemy.

For the next thousand years the bell was heard ringing but its source could never be found. It was said that when the bell rang in the morning it was for joy. Before a storm, the bell warned of the coming danger and before a death it is said that the banshee tolled the bell. If the bell rang at a funeral there was the promise of rest and immortality for the departed soul.

After many centuries the bell suddenly stopped ringing and no one could explain its absence. Future generations became sceptical of the bell's history and the stories attached to it. In 1885, a large oak which stood beside the old church in Kilbroney Cemetery was blown down during a bad storm.

Afterwards workmen started to saw up the old tree. Suddenly they discovered a recess in the trunk and inside was the 'ghostly bell'. They also found the bell's tongue at the bottom of the recess and this explained why the bell was not heard as it had lost its ability to create a sound.

Saint Bronach's Bell is now located in the Catholic Church in Rostrevor.

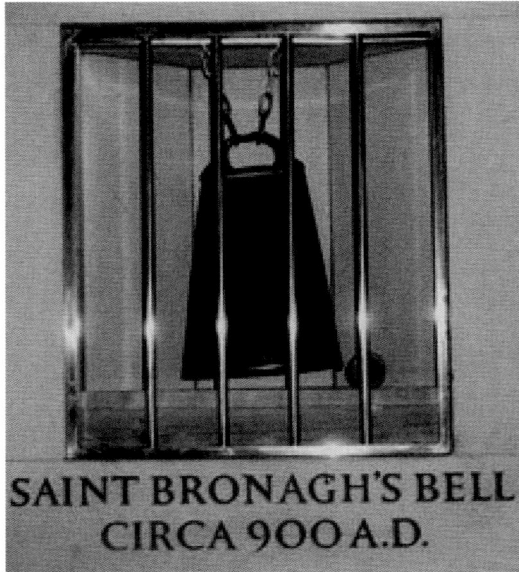

SAINT BRONAGH'S BELL
CIRCA 900 A.D.

The Slieve Binnian Light

In the Mourne area ramblers have to be aware of the Slieve Binnian light. This warns them away from a certain spot, an area of haunted trees near Spelga Dam where it is claimed that a certain Irish Chieftain lies buried.

Lough Shannagh Monster

W D Fitzpatrick tells the story of the most terrible water dragon ever known in Ireland which set up home in Lough Shannagh deep in the Mourne Mountains.

It would devour at least fifty cattle each day and if the local people did not provide this the monster would hunt down and kill every human being it could find. Its presence was causing devastation among the population and all the farms for miles around. One of the local chieftains was called Aidan and he and some of his men were summoned to deal with the monster and to force it to depart. One of Aidan's advisors Ablach volunteered to approach the dragon and find out why it had come to the Mournes and what it would take to get rid of it. As Ablach and his comrades approached the lake, the beast emerged and raised its head from the water letting out a terrible roar.

Ablach understood that the dragon was demanding sixty steeds by sunrise otherwise it would devour all. The Chieftain ordered Ablach to tell the dragon that this wish was impossible and no-one was scared of the dragon anymore. As Ablach relayed the message, he stepped back from the dragon so that he would be a safe distance from its ferocious jaws. However, the dragon was so angry at what he had been told that he opened his huge jaws and with a roaring intake of breath, it sucked Alblach down its throat. It then rolled out of the lake, as it had no limbs and attacked the rest of Aidan's men swallowing them whole.

The chieftain Aidan was enraged by this and raced to the dragon himself throwing himself onto the monster's neck. With all his strength, he twisted and twisted its neck round and round until it was forced to roll over on its back. The monster was then unable to get up. Aidan held firm while his remaining men rushed to the scene and cut open the monsters throat.

Out spilled Ablach and the other warriors the dragon had devoured. They all looked well despite their ordeal. After this the monster was let go and it slid back into the lake where it sank to the bottom like a massive stone. Everyone in the Mournes was overjoyed when they heard that the dragon had been slain. They lit bonfires on all the peaks and celebrated for nine days and nights. Chieftain Aidan and his men were honoured as heroes.

The Legendery Fairy Cat of Clough

This famous beast was reputed to be enormous and acted as a sort of 'guard dog' for the area and when a castle was built in Clough's fairy rath, the cat was put in charge. The local people slept secure at night knowing that their cat would protect them in the event of any danger. The cat was mistaken for a panther in Saxon times. The castle has long since gone and another large house was built in its place. Mountpanther House takes its name from the great cat. Unfortunately this once impressive old house now lies in ruins and is currently up for sale. In 1942, Mount Panther was the home to US soldiers who were based in the area.

Finn McCool Legends in County Down

Finn McCool (Fionn Mac Cumhaill) was well known as a warrior and a giant. Legend has it that Finn once had a long and fierce battle with another giant from the other edge of Carlingford Lough. Finn was situated in the Slieve Foy side while the other giant was now standing on the County Down side. They fought long and hard and while Finn was sleeping, the other giant sneaked over the water and stole Finn's sword. When Finn awoke, he fell in to a great rage and started to throw stones and boulders across the lough.

One stone was the Cloughmore Stone which weighed over 50 tons. With all his strength, Finn managed to throw it across the lough at the other giant. It landed on the unfortunate's head, crushing his great body into the mountain where it melted away like snow beneath the stone.

The Cloughmore Stone still lies above Rostrevor village. It is said that it and other rocks on Slieve Meen originated in the Cooley Mountains which lie on the other side of the lough and vice versa. Walking around the Cloughmore Stone seven times will allegedly bring good luck.

Another legend associated with Finn lies in Seafin Castle (Sidhe Finn meaning the Seat of Finn McCool). It is situated alongside the River Bann in Drumballyroney. It is claimed that Finn and his soldiers often stayed there to rest between their many battles.

One particular story describes how Finn brought a beautiful young lady back to the Castle after one such battle. She had put a spell on Finn and he was completely under her power. His warriors, however, noticed that she took on the appearance of an old witch while she slept. They decided to get rid of her and threw her body in the nearby River Bann. The river bubbled and turned red and black as she disappeared under the water. Some say her reflection can still be seen if one looks closely into the water near the ruined castle.

Seafin Castle near Ballyroney

Chapter 10

Stories from Beyond County Down

The South Armagh Ghost Train

The main Belfast to Dublin train passes through County Down and Armagh before it crosses the border after it leaves Killeen.

Sightings of a strange train began at the early part of this century. One such sighting was by a railway official who lived close to the railway and whose job was to attend one of the gates. As all scheduled trains had passed for the night he was very surprised to hear a train approaching from the North. As it was his duty to be present at the gates with his lamp, he went outside and observed the passenger train emerging from 'The Wellington Cutting' in Killeen but when it travelled on to a place called 'Barney's Bridge' it suddenly disappeared! He walked to bridge but could see nothing.

The next day the railway man relayed his story and other people also admitted that they also had heard the ghost train and it stopping at Barney's Bridge. The railway man's cottage became the centre of attention and many people gathered there at night to wait for the train to pass again. Their patience was eventually rewarded and one night after all the scheduled trains had gone, another train was heard approaching. The gateman went outside with his lamp while others remained inside and looked out of the window. Everyone was amazed to see the lighted carriages of the train emerging from the cutting and then disappear at the bridge.

Those who believe in ghosts maintain that most sightings are connected with a tragic event that occurred in that particular place. In this area, the most tragic railway disaster ever to occur in Ireland took place a short distance from where the sightings were reported.

One June morning in 1889, a busy train set out from Armagh to Warrenpoint. The passengers included children who were on their annual excursion with the Methodist Church. It is estimated that there were up to twelve hundred people on board. The train struggled to climb the hill and it stopped as the engine was unable to deal with the heavy load. It was decided to split the train in two, bringing one half of the carriages over the hill and then coming back for the other ones. Stones were placed under the wheels of the back carriages to prevent them rolling backwards.

When the engine once again started, it suddenly jerked backwards and crashed into the back carriages. The stones underneath the wheels were crushed and the back carriages started to move backwards down the hill picking up speed as they descended. Some passengers managed to jump clear but many of the doors were locked as there were so many children on board. Those on board were terrified especially so when they observed another train coming.

There was a massive collision. Many carriages were smashed to pieces and the engine of the oncoming train was thrown aside like a little toy. Meanwhile the front end of the first train was also rolling back when one of the railway men managed to apply the hand brakes. He was badly injured in the process and died later. So many men, women and children were killed and badly injured as a result of the crash. Dead bodies littered the embankment and the injured were heard screaming from inside the trains. The disaster sent shock waves throughout the country and the final death toll was eighty eight.

Many argue that the sighting of the ghost train is connected with this disaster as they occurred in the same area.

Greenaway's Ghost in Portadown

Many years ago in Portadown, John Greenaway was a local councillor and ran a boot and shoe shop in Morley Street. He often told the story of how he would be woken at night by the sound of tongs rattling in the fire grate. The next morning he would find ashes scattered all over the floor yet no-one else was in the house apart from himself and his wife. The local doctor also noticed bruises on Mrs Greenaway's body where she had been crushed against the bannisters by an invisible force as she went down to the basement. Other strange stories involved the grandfather clock suddenly starting to chime during the night. It would only be silenced if someone manually removed the weight.

Many of John's customers found that boxes of shoes were often mixed up with different colours and sizes in the same box with no explanation. A local teacher visited the house and while they were discussing books, he went to the bookcase to reach for a copy of R. L Stevenson's 'Kidnapped'. Just before he lifted the book, a cold wind swept through the room and all the books tumbled down off the bookcase and fell on the floor - that is all except one. The remaining book was 'Kidnapped'.

Greenaway's Ghost in Portadown

The family decided to carry out an exorcism in the house and the ghost was trapped inside a bottle by the local priest. The bottle itself was hidden close by. Children were, however, still frightened to go near the house as it was said that some nights the ghost in the bottle could be heard screaming to get out.

Lurgan Woman Was Buried Twice

The fear of being buried alive is a real one and became a reality for a young Lurgan woman called Marjorie McCall back in 1705. In those days, graves were often dug up so that the robbers would remove any valuables such as jewellery from the bodies.

Although her husband was a type of surgeon, after she became ill and unconscious, her family declared that she was dead. At her wake, many tried to remove a valuable ring which she always wore but it could not be removed. Anyway, she was buried in Shankhill Graveyard and that very night her body was exhumed by robbers who were after her ring.

They also could not remove the ring and decided to cut off her finger. As soon as blood was drawn from poor Marjorie, she woke from her coma. The robbers were so frightened that they ran from the graveyard and never looked back. Marjorie managed to climb out of the grave and made her way home.

Her family were all gathered around the fire at her house to keep her husband company after his sad loss. Marjorie knocked at the door. Her husband declared *"If your mother was still alive, I'd swear that was her knock"*. And sure enough, when he opened the door, he saw his wife, dressed in her burial clothes and very much alive. He then fainted on the spot.

It is reported that Marjorie lived for some years after this event and when she did die she was buried once again in Shankill Graveyard. Her gravestone exists today and bears the inscription

'Lived Once, Buried Twice'

The headstone of Marjorie McCall in Lurgan

In Bed with a Ghost, Belfast & Loughinisland

This was probably one of the most interesting stories we came across during our research. It was about a ghost that followed a family even when they moved house to a different part of the country. It all started in a house located in Stockmans Lane in Belfast. The occupants of the house had a small child and it would waken at the exact time every night as if it had a nightmare. The mother described how she could have timed to the very minute each night at 3am when the child would wake out of its sleep screaming with terror. It would take a half an hour or more to get it settled again.

On another occasion the father was in the child's room and suddenly he noticed a figure standing at the door. He walked towards it and kicked out at the figure but there was nothing there. He turned on the light and it was gone. Then it felt as if a cloud of smoke had went into his mouth. The man found the whole experience very surreal and could not understand what it was.

The couple decided to leave the house and move to Loughinisland because they felt the house in Belfast had a presence which may not have wanted them there. However, the ghost seemed to follow them because within a few weeks of moving, the strangest thing of all happened. One night the man was out for the night playing music and he was staying with a friend in Castlewellan. During the night his wife was lying in the bed and she felt a tug on the quilt. She thought it was her husband and said, *"I thought you said you weren't coming home tonight!"* She felt as if a full size body was lying beside her but there was no warmth coming from it. The woman turned around to see why she had not heard an answer and was shocked to see that there was no one there.

The couple were running out of options and as a last resort, decided to call on the services of a medium to visit their home and try to communicate with the spirit. The medium told them to imagine a gold or silver thread wrapping itself into a cocoon right in the centre of their eyes. Then they had to say the words *"I don't need you here and I don't want you here!"* They had to repeat this phrase three times. After this, the couple never had any more encounters with the ghost. The medium was able to tell them that the ghost was the man's father who had died a few years previous and that he only wanted to make sure that they were alright. Strangely enough, after its departure, the woman found it quite lonely not having the spirit in the house because she was so used to its presence.

Haunted Police Station, Belfast

The old police station on Queen's Street in Belfast is widely known for being haunted and many unexplained things have happened there over the years. One night in late December

2013 a group of people who were sceptical of the stories decided to visit the site and spend the night in it. What happened that night was quite peculiar.

They heard footsteps walking towards them and then suddenly part of the ceiling collapsed in the next room. It was clear to the individuals that the spirit did not like their presence and it may have been some form of poltergeist. The exact same noise was heard again in the room a few minutes later. When the people examined the ceiling it was already completely collapsed many years previously so no-one could explain the noise. As they shone their touch around the room they also noticed that there was no dust coming from the rubble on the ground. The legend has it that someone had fallen through the ceiling after the police station closed down and was killed instantly. Its ghost apparently returns to re-enact this terrible tragedy and appears to be very aggressive.

The group were actually videoing when it happened a third time but once again there was nothing to be seen. It sounded as if there were footsteps or someone walking just before it happened. They asked the spirit to speak to them and it said its name was Andrew. Then there was another large bang. Following this another ghost made contact with them in a different part of the building. He informed them that he was a soldier and his name was Steven.

Molly the Friendly Ghost, Lisburn

This story begins in 1980 when a man, his wife and three children aged 9yrs, 8yrs and 6yrs moved to a grand 2 storey four bed, terrace house in Llewellyn Avenue, on the Belfast Road, Lisburn. These houses were built in 1906 and had two bedrooms on the top floor, two in the middle floor and a bathroom and toilet to the rear along a long landing. Downstairs consisted of a hallway, stairs, two good sized living rooms and a long dining / kitchen area to the rear. The family had only moved in about two weeks when some very strange, unexplained things started to happen. Their 8 year old daughter said she had seen an elderly lady on the first floor landing. She had a long dress on and was smiling. The young girl was not frightened at all.

A few days later the family were rushing out of the house for an appointment. The children were in the car and the mother was just after changing into a skirt when she noticed the stitching along the side of the zipper was ripped. She took it off and put it over the banister stating *"I'll repair that later"* and changed into another skirt. On their return later that evening she found the stitching along the zipper intact. Someone had fixed it while they were away.

The family had a little Yorkshire terrier dog at that time and in the evenings the dog was always downstairs. It is said that dogs have an instinct or senses for things unseen, so the father watched the dog's reaction when strange noises occurred inside the house. She pricked her ears up at the cubby-hole door under the stairs on several occasions. When the man opened the door she never would go in as if it was afraid to go any further. It also barked with a strange growl.

On another occasion, the father was decorating his bedroom and worked until late in the evening. He got washed, changed for bed and checked the children who were all fast asleep in their beds on the top floor. He turned off the light on the landing and went back into his bedroom. As he got into bed beside his wife he could see the reflection of the landing light coming on again in the mirror above the dressing table. It gave him a quite a fright because he knew it could not have been any of the children or his wife who had turned it on. The landing light remained on every night for the next three years even though it had been turned off.

On two different occasions as the parents were in bed, they both heard the noise of knives and forks being rattled in the kitchen. The couple's fourth child was a son, born in 1983 and he was only a few months old when the mother got the fright of her life. One morning about 11am, she was alone downstairs in the house when she heard what seemed like the loud noise of curtains being swished to and fro and coming from one of the bedrooms. The young child was asleep in that bedroom. A neighbour was called upon to assist and both went upstairs and found the child had slept through the noises. A voice could then he heard and it said, *"I am Molly and I'm not here to hurt you!"*

The strangest occurrence of all was on the night they were leaving to move to a new home in Banbridge. It was early December 1983 and almost all their belongings had been moved to the new house. It was dark and snowing and they had just placed the last few items in the car. One of the neighbours called to help with the final packing and as they were chatting about the strange happenings in the house, the water pipes suddenly started to rattle throughout the whole house for about five minutes. The noise continued as they pulled the front door closed behind them. A lady's voice could be heard saying *"Goodbye, I will miss you!"*

None of the family was really frightened by the goings on in that house. Later the man spoke to the new owners of the house and enquired if they had experienced anything strange but they had not.

Bibliography

As I Roved Out by Cathal O' Byrne, Lagan Books 2000.

Down Folk Tales by Steve Lally. The History Press, Ireland, 2013.

Growing Up In Portadown in the Thirties and Forties by Harry Foy.

Irish Fairy Tales, Retold by Philip Wilson. Tara 1999.

Journal of the Upper Ards Historical Society, No. 20, 1996.

Legendary Stories of The Carlingford Lough District (Centenary Edition 1913-2013), Michael G. Crawford. Reprinted by WG Baird Limited 2012. Published by the M Havern Family, Warrenpoint.

Tales and Legends of Lecale by T.M. Tate.

The Phantom Football Match by W. J. Fitzpatrick.

The Encylopedia of Ghosts and Spirits by John and Anne Spencer, Headline Book Publishing PLC, 1992.

True Irish Ghost Stories by John Seymour & Harry Nelligan, Senate Press 1994.

Ulster Folk Lore by Elizabeth Andrews, FRAI, 1913.

Ulster Ghost Stories, Joe Baker and Michael Liggett, Glenravel Publications.

Unexplained Encounters, Exploring the Paranormal in Ulster, Sheila St. Clair. The White Row Press, 2001.

Newspapers

The Newry Reporter

The Mourne Observer

The Down Recorder

Web Pages

www.fairylist.com

www.ghostsearchersireland.com

www.loughcuan.com

www.newryjournal.co.uk

www.carlingfordandmourne.com/myths-and-legends.com

Contributors

Jim Brennan

Padráigín Carson

Clare & Catherine Cull/The Cull Family

Paddy Devlin

Angela Dillon

Joe Evans

John Farrell

Tony Higgins

Vivien Gamble

Joe Greaves

Stevie Hamilton

Steve Lally

Mary Mackin

Patricia Magennis

Shane Milligan

Damien Morgan

Raymond Morris

P J McClean

Seamus McClean

Paddy-Joe & Thomas McClory

Irene McGrady

Tommy McGrady

Tommy O'Hagan

Mick O' Sullivan

Brian & Maureen Quinn

Tommy Rooney

Paul Smylie

Greg Thompson

John Timmins

Carol & Tom Topping

Brian Wallace

Michael Wallace (SNR)

Ruth Weir